The light glittered in Nathan's eyes as his knuckles lightly grazed her cheek. "I'm going to kiss you."

"Do you really think that's a good idea—"

"No. But all night I haven't been able to take my eyes off you. I want to see how that sexy, sassy, smart mouth tastes."

Her heart started to pound until she thought it would jump right out of her chest. "Oh, my—"

"I can't help it." He tucked a strand of hair behind her ear with a shaking hand. "I want to feel all the passion you put into being so tough."

Words were trapped in Cindy's throat so she started to shake her head. The feel of his lips stopped her as surely as it shut down all rational thought....

Dear Reader,

I love fairy tales and have since I was a little girl. *Sleeping Beauty. Cinderella. Beauty and the Beast.* It wasn't clear then, but reading those classics was the foundation for my career as a romance writer now.

I had so much fun tweaking the fairy-tale elements in *Cindy's Doctor Charming.* The "ball" where she first talks to her hero is the beginning of the story, not the end. And, as every woman knows, the perfect fit of a shoe is worth its weight in happily-ever-afters. But for Cindy and Nathan it's the broken heel on her borrowed pumps that allows fate to catch up and bring these two lonely people together in a way neither of them expects.

I hope you enjoy reading their story as much as I enjoyed writing it.

All the best,

Teresa Southwick

P.S. I love to hear from readers. Feel free to contact me through my website at www.teresasouthwick.com.

CINDY'S DOCTOR CHARMING

TERESA SOUTHWICK

SPECIAL EDITION*

Published by Silhouette Books

America's Publisher of Contemporary Romance

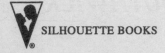

SILHOUETTE BOOKS

ISBN-13: 978-0-373-65579-3

Recycling programs for this product may not exist in your area.

CINDY'S DOCTOR CHARMING

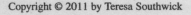

Visit Silhouette Books at www.eHarlequin.com

Printed in U.S.A.

Books by Teresa Southwick

Silhouette Special Edition

†*The Summer House* #1510
  "Courting Cassandra"
†*Midnight, Moonlight & Miracles* #1517
§*It Takes Three* #1631
§*The Beauty Queen's Makeover* #1699
§§*At the Millionaire's Request* #1769
§§*Paging Dr. Daddy* #1886
‡*The Millionaire and the M.D.* #1894
‡*When a Hero Comes Along* #1905
‡*Expecting the Doctor's Baby* #1924
‡‡*Marrying the Virgin Nanny* #1960
‡*The Doctor's Secret Baby* #1982
‡‡*The Nanny and Me* #2001
~~*Taming the Montana Millionaire* #2059
‡*The Surgeon's Favorite Nurse* #2067
‡*Cindy's Doctor Charming* #2097

Silhouette Books

*The Fortunes of Texas:
  Shotgun Vows*

Silhouette Romance

And Then He Kissed Me #1405
With a Little T.L.C. #1421
The Acquired Bride #1474
Secret Ingredient: Love #1495
The Last Marchetti Bachelor #1513
**Crazy for Lovin' You* #1529
**This Kiss* #1541
**If You Don't Know by Now* #1560
**What If We Fall in Love?* #1572
Sky Full of Promise #1624
†*To Catch a Sheik* #1674
†*To Kiss a Sheik* #1686
†*To Wed a Sheik* #1696
††*Baby, Oh Baby* #1704
††*Flirting with the Boss* #1708
††*An Heiress on His
  Doorstep* #1712

§*That Touch of Pink* #1799
§*In Good Company* #1807
§*Something's Gotta Give* #1815

*The Marchetti Family
**Destiny, Texas
†Desert Brides
††If Wishes Were…
§Buy-a-Guy
§§The Wilder Family
‡Men of Mercy Medical
‡‡The Nanny Network
~~Montana Mavericks:
  Thunder Canyon Cowboys

TERESA SOUTHWICK

lives with her husband in Las Vegas, the city that reinvents itself every day. An avid fan of romance novels, she is delighted to be living out her dream of writing for Silhouette Books.

To all of you who love happy endings as much as I do.

Chapter One

She was a fake and a fraud.

Cindy Elliott was walking, talking, breathing proof that not only was it possible to make a silk purse from a sow's ear, but you also could take her out in public. So far no one had pointed and laughed at her pretending to be one of the exalted affluent. But the night was young and she was the queen of getting dumped on.

Famous-rich and anonymous-wealthy people were crammed into this ballroom. She was pretty sure that, unlike herself, none of them had won their seat at this thousand-dollar-a-plate fundraiser with a raffle ticket. Any second she expected the riffraff police to see through her disguise and throw her out.

It wouldn't be the worst thing that ever happened to her, but it was not high on her list of things to do. Her plan was to enjoy every moment of this night. Take in every detail and let the memories brighten the daily grind as she dug herself out of the deep financial hole she'd ended up in after trusting a man.

Cindy grew up in Las Vegas but this was the first time she'd ever been to a shindig at Caesar's Palace. Crystal chandeliers glittered overhead and silver light trickled down on white tablecloths and somehow made the fragrant arrangements of fresh, vibrantly colored flowers smell even better. Candles flickered but paled in comparison to the views visible from floor-to-ceiling windows of the neon skyline outside on the Strip.

She wished more people were looking at *it* instead of her, more specifically male people. A lot of the dapper men in dark suits and tuxedos were staring at her as she snaked her way through the crush of bodies. She felt conspicuous and self-conscious in her strapless, champagne-colored cocktail dress. It was knee length, and now was not a good time to wish for more material.

Finally she reached the perimeter of the room and found the table number that corresponded to the one on her invitation. There were eight chairs and all of them were empty. She decided to sit down and take the strain off her borrowed shoes, minding her friend's warning not to test the limits of a Super Glue repair on a four-inch heel.

Moments later someone appeared in her peripheral vision and a familiar deep voice said, "Is this seat taken?"

Cindy looked up. The face matched the voice as she'd feared it would. Nathan Steele, MD. Dr. Charming himself, she thought sarcastically. He always made her think of Hugh Jackman—tall and broad-shouldered, with hazel eyes and dark brown hair. It pained her to admit, even to herself, that his traditional black tuxedo made him look very handsome—for a bad-tempered, arrogant, egotistical physician.

After a couple seconds of him standing there expectantly,

the message translated from her eyes to her brain that he was waiting for an answer. Glancing at the seven empty seats, she briefly thought about saying that her date was sitting there, then abandoned the idea. She might be a pathetic loser who was a really bad judge of men, but she wasn't a liar.

"No," she finally said. "That seat isn't taken."

He smiled, then lowered his excellent butt into the chair beside hers. "Isn't that lucky?"

"You have no idea." She looked at him, waiting for the inevitable moment when he recognized her as the incompetent from Mercy Medical Center's housekeeping department. The same employee he'd chastised earlier that day for something that wasn't her fault. The indignity and unfairness still smarted.

"Would you like a drink?" The tone was pleasant, deep and sexy. Definitely not his icy-cold, all-business hospital voice.

"Yes." It was the least he could do. "A glass of red wine would be lovely."

He stood. "Don't let anyone take this seat."

"I wouldn't dream of it."

Dream being the operative word. Nathan Steele was walking, talking female fantasy. Definite hero material. A handsome doctor whose mission in life was to save babies who came into this world too early. Infants who needed every trick in his medical bag to survive outside a mother's protective womb while their not-ready-to-be born bodies caught up. How could a woman not seriously crush on a man like that?

The answer was simple. Pretty to look at, difficult to get along with. Cindy didn't need the aggravation. She was still paying for the last wrong guy at the wrong time. She was a twenty-seven-year-old college student because she'd lost not only her bank account but money she hadn't even earned yet to a good-looking man masquerading as a hero. She literally couldn't afford another stupid man mistake.

A few minutes later Dr. Charming set a glass of red wine in front of her and a whiskey neat at his own place before settling beside her again.

"I'm Dr. Steele—Nathan." He looked at her, obviously waiting for her to respond with an introduction. When she said nothing, he added, "And you are?"

Surprised and annoyed in equal parts, she thought. The fact that he didn't recognize her was a surprise. It also annoyed her.

"Cindy Elliott," she said, waiting for the "aha" light to shine in his eyes.

"Nice to meet you, Cindy." He held his hand out.

She wanted to tell him they'd already met. More than once their paths had crossed in the hospital. But then she put her fingers into his palm and a ripple of awareness danced up her arm. He held babies weighing hardly more than a pound, tiny little things that easily fit into this hand. It was warm and strong and capable.

Hero worship threatened until she remembered that doing battle for babies barely alive didn't give him license to be a bastard to everyone else.

"Dr. Steele," she said with as much cool reserve as she could muster.

"Call me Nathan."

"All right. Nathan."

He studied her intently and finally said, "Where do I know you from?"

It was on the tip of her tongue to say she saw him almost every day. Granted, the disposable, white "bunny suit" she wore for her housekeeping job in the neonatal intensive care unit made her fairly anonymous. But still...

She was about to tell him, then something stopped her. The devil made her do it. "I look familiar?"

"Yes."

Maybe she'd finally caught a break. "I guess I just have one of those faces."

"Quite a lovely face."

And now it was red. How did she respond to that? "Thank you."

"I can't shake the feeling that we've met." He sipped his drink. "Did you have a baby in the NICU?"

Heaven forbid. A baby was the last thing she needed. Although that would require sex and she hadn't had any for a very long time. "I've never had a baby."

"So you're here at the fundraiser out of the goodness of your heart?"

"I won a seat at the table with a raffle ticket," she said honestly.

"Right." His mouth curved up at the corners.

"I'm not kidding." The amused expression on his face said he didn't believe her. Honesty was always the best policy. "There's no way I could afford to come to something like this otherwise."

"Of course." His gaze lowered to the spot where the champagne-colored piping on her dress criss-crossed over her breasts. For a moment, intensity flared in his eyes and then amusement returned. "Raffle ticket. If I had a nickel for every time I heard that."

"It's the absolute truth."

"Uh huh. Who's your stylist?"

Stylist? She almost laughed. No way could she afford something like that. "Not a stylist. They're called friends. Fairy godmothers."

"So they pulled off a miracle with a magic wand?" One dark eyebrow rose.

"As a matter of fact…" She took a sip of wine and warmed to the subject. "I wasn't going to come, but my friends talked me into it. I borrowed the dress, shoes and bag from Flora, Fauna and Merryweather."

"Who?"

"They're characters from an animated fairy tale. Surely you saw it when you were a kid."

He shook his head and all hint of laughter disappeared. "No."

"You probably don't remember. It's a classic children's movie."

"That explains it. I was never a child."

The sort of lost expression on his face pulled at her heart and she fought the feeling down, mentally stomped the stuffing out of it. Life was hard and then you met someone who made things harder. Not happening to her again. "I don't know what to say to that."

"It doesn't require a response." He shrugged. "Just a fact."

"Sad fact." Those were two words she wanted back. He didn't need her sympathy and she didn't want to feel sorry for him. But tell that to her bleeding heart, which always got her into trouble. *Used* to get her in trouble. Past tense. She was a reformed soft touch.

"What was your childhood like?" he asked.

"There wasn't a lot of money, but my brother and I didn't know anything different." She thought back to the time before her mother died. "We hung out with friends. Had sleepovers. Pizza and movies. Carefree."

He nodded. "Sounds nice."

"It was." She was going to be sorry for asking, but she couldn't stop herself. "What was yours like? You might not have thought you were a child but everyone starts out that way."

"I was more what you'd call an unaccompanied minor." He took a sip from his glass and drained the contents. "On my own a lot."

"Only child?"

He nodded. "You had a brother?"

"Still do. He's in college. In California." And she was struggling to keep him there because it was her fault the money her father had saved for his education was gone. "I miss him."

"And that detour into childhood was really off the subject." His puzzled expression was back.

"What subject would that be?" The question was just a stall. She should just tell him that he knew her from the hospital. She worked in housekeeping. But some perverse part of her wanted a little payback for his earlier temper tantrum.

"Who are you?"

"Cindy Elliott," she answered.

"So you said." He studied her face until shivers of awareness made her want to squirm. Finally he shook his head. "But I still can't figure out why I know you. Where do you work?"

"Mercy Medical Center." That would jog his memory. Again she waited for the "aha" moment.

"Really?" Instead of recognition, his puzzled frown deepened. "What department?"

"Guess." She took a large swallow of wine.

"Nursing."

She shook her head.

"Human Resources?"

"No." She twirled the long stem of the glass on the table in front of her.

"Dietary?"

"You mean Nutritional Services?" she asked.

"That was politically incorrect of me. Yes, that's what I meant."

She shook her head. "Nope, don't work there either."

"Okay. I give up."

"All evidence to the contrary." If he gave up that easily, there were a lot of babies who wouldn't be alive today. Welcome to a classic conundrum. She was invisible to him. In all fairness, at the hospital he was totally focused on his tiny patients and got points for that. But he'd actually talked to her, chastised her really, for something she hadn't done. How could she admire him so much at the same time she found him to be a pain in the neck?

"What does that mean?" he asked.

That she was an idiot. "I've seen you in action in the NICU."

"But you're not a nurse."

"I'm an administrative intern at Mercy Medical Center. In addition to—other things," she said vaguely.

Before he could answer, an announcement was made for everyone to find their tables and the program would begin. Cindy was grateful for the distraction as the seats around them were filled and introductions made. She talked to the people on her right and tried to ignore the man on her left. Not so easy when their shoulders brushed and thighs bumped. Every stroke sent a surge of heat through her.

She smiled politely, laughed when appropriate and planned to slip out at the first opportunity.

Nathan had expected this dinner to be acutely boring speeches and barely edible rubber chicken. A yawn. He'd been wrong. Not about the speeches and chicken. But he'd never felt less like yawning.

That was because of the mysterious Cindy Elliott.

The words from a song came to mind, about seeing a

stranger across a crowded room. The shimmer of her blond hair had first caught his attention. Her slender curves in the strapless, shiny beige dress were sexy and so damn hot he needed about an hour in a subzero shower.

He'd have followed her anywhere, but when she sat at his table, he wondered if somehow the god of luck had finally come down on his side. The certainty that he'd seen her somewhere now seemed less important than getting her attention away from the woman she'd been talking to on her right side. All through the endless meal she'd industriously ignored him and that was about to end. A quartet had set up to play music and people were moving to the wooden dance floor in the center of the room.

Finally there was a break in the gabfest. He leaned close and said near her ear, "Would you like to dance?"

She met his gaze for several moments and finally said, "I don't think so."

It wasn't ego that caused his surprise at the smackdown. It was that women simply didn't do that. He was forever being introduced by matchmaking mothers who were trying to hook up the successful doctor with their daughter or niece. Or a friend's daughter or niece. Or second cousin once removed. Women liked him. And he liked women.

There was never a challenge involved. He rubbed his neck as that sank in. Maybe there *was* a little ego mixed in with the surprise.

"Why?" he finally asked.

"Why what?"

"Don't you want to dance?"

Her eyes narrowed. They were the color of cinnamon and snapping with intelligence. He found himself eagerly anticipating her response.

"I need a reason?"

"It would be polite."

"Not if I had to explain about a prosthetic leg. Or a pronounced limp from a serious childhood soccer injury."

Like almost every other man in the room, he'd watched the sexy sway of her hips as she'd glided gracefully to the table. The only imminent injury was the rising level of testosterone threatening to blow the top of his head off.

"Do you have any physical limitations?" he asked.

"No."

"Okay." Before she made him navigate more speed bumps, he said, "And you know how to dance?"

"See, that's the thing. Mumsy and Daddy begged me to go to cotillion to smooth out my rough edges—"

"Mumsy?"

She smiled. "Yes. My über-wealthy parents desperately wanted to be here tonight but they simply couldn't tear themselves away from the south of France."

"Über-wealthy?" That's not what she'd told him before. "Just exactly how much did you pay for that lucky raffle ticket?"

Amusement curved the corners of her full, tempting lips. "So you actually were paying attention."

"It's part of my charm."

"Oh, please. Do women really fall for that line?"

"Yes. Although usually a line isn't involved."

"It's a darn shame." She eased away, a pitying expression on her face.

"What?"

"You should really do something about your self-confidence. Surgery. Rehab. There must be some treatment. The miracles of modern medicine—"

"Aren't miracles," he finished.

"No?"

"It's science."

"Really?" There was a spark of interest now.

"Absolutely."

"You don't believe in miracles?" She rested her arm on the table as she angled her body toward him.

"I never underestimate the power of the human spirit. But a miracle?" He shook his head. "If I can't see or touch it, I don't believe it exists."

"What about love?"

Oddly enough, he was pretty sure the question wasn't Cindy being flirtatious. If an invitation to his bed was her goal, she'd be in his arms on the dance floor right now. Instead of having her soft curves pressed against him and the scent of her skin snarling his senses, they were having an existential discussion regarding the reality of love.

"I don't believe in it."

"You're kidding, right?" she asked.

"No."

In the NICU he'd seen worried parents who almost literally willed a tiny scrap of humanity born too soon, a being that they'd only just met face to face, to live. Was that love? He didn't know. It hadn't existed in his life. There'd been buckets of money that his father spent copious amounts of time making. His mother got tired of trying to get her husband's attention and turned to her "projects."

Nathan had tried his hand at love. He'd married a woman he liked and respected. But there was no doubt in his mind that if she hadn't died in a car accident, their trial separation would have turned into an amicable divorce. He missed her, as his best friend. Nothing deeper than that existed in his world. He had no frame of reference for love.

Enough with the self-examination, he thought. He was a doctor, trained to act swiftly and decisively in an emergency. Hesitation could cost lives. And as Cindy had pointed out, his self-confidence needed immediate resuscitation.

He stood, then took her hand and pulled her to her feet. "We're wasting a perfectly good waltz."

He'd expected some rebellion in the ranks, but apparently he had surprise on his side. She didn't pull away but followed almost meekly as he led her through the maze of tables littered with half-eaten cheesecake and hastily abandoned cloth napkins.

On the dance floor he slid his arm around her waist and nestled her against him. She wasn't as tall as he'd thought. It was probably that big attitude of hers generating the illusion. He was used to willowy women, but he could rest his chin on the top of Cindy's head and somehow the fit felt just right. Despite her tongue-in-cheek comments about prosthetics and pronounced limps, she was light on her feet and had no problem following his lead. It felt as if they'd been dancing together for years.

Nathan gave brief thought to making conversation, then decided if he kept his mouth shut, he couldn't put his foot in it. The sweet fragrance of her skin filled his head, more intoxicating than any alcohol he'd ever tasted. Thoughts of her in his arms somewhere private, with the sexy, strapless dress on the floor around her feet was temptation with a capital *T*. He was already planning the strategy to make that happen because it had been hard enough to get her in his arms for a dance.

The music ended and he was about to make his pitch when she backed away. The almost stricken expression on her face puzzled him.

"What's wrong?"

"Nothing. I have to go."

"It's not late," he protested.

"It is for me."

"Don't tell me," he said. "Your car turns into a pumpkin at midnight."

"Something like that." She did an about-face, then slipped away through the crush of bodies still on the dance floor.

"Wait." He knew she heard, because she lifted her hand in a wave as she kept going.

The crowd was thinner than when he'd first arrived tonight, but he had trouble maintaining a visual of her. She kept disappearing because almost everyone was taller. Outside the ballroom in the wide, carpeted hall people milled around. Nathan looked left, then right and couldn't see her.

Instinct had him hurrying toward the bank of escalators leading to the ground level. When he reached the bottom, the crush of bodies parted and there she was, one foot bare and holding a high-heeled pump in her hand. The heel dangled at a dangerous angle. Literally a lucky break for him.

"Looks like you could use some help."

She looked up, her expression rueful. "Not unless you can surgically reattach this."

"I could carry you," he suggested.

She made a great show of assessing him from the chest up. "You probably could. And that would be very gallant. But I wouldn't try it if I were you." Despite the spunky words, she put her hand on his arm for balance as she removed the other shoe.

"So you're determined to go?"

"Even more now." The look she turned on him was wry. "I have no shoes."

"Not a problem for me."

"That makes one of us," she said.

"Okay. I'll let you go quietly if you give me your phone number."

She blinked up at him, and for a split second the idea

seemed to tempt her. Then she shook her head. "I don't think that's a very good idea."

"You don't want me to call you?"

"Give the man a gold star." Regret flickered in her eyes although she probably didn't know it was there. "It's not that I don't appreciate the interest, but women like me don't date men like you."

"I have no idea what that means."

"Okay, how about this? My parents aren't in the south of France or even north Las Vegas for that matter. It was the truth when I told you there's no money in my family."

"I believe you. That's not why—"

"Look Dr. Can't-take-no-for-an-answer. I don't want you to call me. You're a jerk at work. You yell at the help. You have a terrible reputation and no one likes you, including me. And everyone thinks you're inflexible."

He laughed. "You're going to have to do better than that."

"No, I really don't."

"If it's not already clear, *I'd* like to see *you* again."

Something flashed in her eyes when she said "Yeah, well, we all want things we can't have."

Before he could stop her, she turned and vanished in the crowd, ending his lucky streak. The most interesting woman he'd ever met had just shut him down.

At least he knew her name. It was a place to start.

Chapter Two

Tired and cranky the morning after her big night, Cindy and her "clean cart" rode the elevator to Mercy Medical Center's second floor. If she'd known her raffle ticket to the ball included a sleepless night because of Dr. Charming, spending the evening at home in her slippers and sweats would have won out over borrowed finery and broken heels. She still couldn't believe that Nathan Steele, the legendary NICU doc, had asked for her phone number. If he'd known she worked in housekeeping at the hospital, the fairy tale would certainly have ended differently.

The elevator arrived at her stop and the doors whispered open. She pushed the cart, holding a mop, trash receptacle and trigger bottles filled with antiseptic spray, down the hall. After rounding the corner, she came to a screeching halt. Nathan was standing right outside the neonatal intensive care unit.

He was looking at his phone, probably a BlackBerry or

whatever was the latest expensive communication technology crammed into a square case barely visible to the naked eye. She wouldn't know. Her cell phone was old, her calling plan the cheapest available on the market, only for emergencies. Which running into Dr. Steele definitely was, but nothing an old, cheap cell phone could handle.

The good news was that he hadn't seen her yet. She could turn around and hide someplace until he was gone, but there was work to do. She was already gowned in the white, paper coverall with the snaps marching up the front that the unit required. Except for the disposable blue booties over her sneakers, she looked like a bunny. If only this uniform included a bag to put over her head, he wouldn't know her because her ID badge was hidden beneath the protective clothing.

Then she got a grip and realized he overlooked her on a daily basis. There was no reason to believe that had changed because the night before he'd flirted with her outrageously and asked a woman he didn't recognize for her number. The dancing had been really nice, too.

With head held high, she walked past him and stopped at the double-door entrance to the NICU. The cart wasn't allowed inside. With all the sensitive equipment, electrical cords and highly skilled personnel hurrying between the isolettes, there wasn't room to spare for the clunky cart. Housekeeping paraphernalia was necessary but not even in the same league with the pricey, sensitive and technical tools that saved the babies.

Cindy picked up one of the trigger bottles and was just about to approach the automatic opening door when she felt someone behind her. The hair at her nape prickled and her skin flushed with heat that had nothing to do with the hot suit. She could be wrong about the awareness, but she was pretty sure she wasn't. The same thing had happened once before. Specifically, last night.

"Cindy?"

It was *him*. Not only that, he'd called her by name and as far as she knew he hadn't looked at her. She turned, bracing for this unprecedented happening. And there was Dr. Charming with his meticulously mussed hair and swoon-worthy square jaw. He was dressed in scrubs, which weren't particularly appealing, except that he was wearing them.

"How did you know it was me?" she asked.

"I recognized your perfume."

Well, damn. Why did he have to be a smooth talker on top of everything else? "I don't know what to say to that."

"Interesting development because last night you had all the answers."

If he really believed that, she'd put on a pretty good performance. "About that—"

"So this is where I know you from."

"Scene of the crime." She'd let him connect whatever dots he saw fit to explain why she'd made him guess her identity.

"Crime being the pertinent word. It wasn't my finest hour. I owe you an apology."

At the speed of light he'd figured out that she was the housekeeper he'd chastised the day before. Pigs must be flying outside the window because this was an unexpected and unprecedented turn of events.

Doctors never apologized to housekeepers, partly because they were the ones who cleaned up after the high and mighty and just disappeared into the landscape.

"Excuse me, but I could have sworn you used the word *apology*."

"I suppose your hostility is logical."

"Really? You think?" She rested her free hand on her hip. "Maybe because I was found guilty without benefit of a fair trial? I didn't touch that baby in the NICU."

He nodded. "I saw movement. It was a peripheral vision thing—"

"NICU housekeeping 101—never touch the babies. Stifle any rogue maternal instincts and beat them into submission. It was the first thing I was taught and I learned my lesson well."

"There's a good reason for the rule. The babies are incredibly fragile. It's tempting to want to hold them because the heat shield on the Giraffe is up. For a good reason. The neonates need a lot of attention and we need fast and easy access to them."

She knew the Giraffe was the commonly used nickname for the highly specialized isolette that could move up, down and other directions just by pushing a button.

"I know how frail they are," she said. "I understand that the goal is to keep the environment like a mother's womb, warm and quiet. And that begs the question—If calm is what you want, why did you yell at me?"

"Technically, I didn't yell. My tone was moderated. At best, forceful." Her exaggerated eye roll didn't stop him. "And I pulled you aside to the nurse's station, away from the baby."

"And that makes it so much better," she said, lifting the floodgates on her sarcasm. "That way the nurses could really hear you unreasonably humiliate me."

"It was an overreaction." His hazel eyes turned more gold than green and went all puppy dog. "Would it help to explain that the little guy was just born? He weighs a little more than three pounds and it's touch and go. I was worried and took it out on you."

"That's something I never got from the job description

or orientation. Nowhere in my employee handbook does it say that my function is to absorb a physician's deflected tension or anger." She could tell he was listening and letting her vent, but that didn't sit well or turn off the mad. "Housekeepers aren't here to be stress relievers for anyone higher up on the food chain."

He really looked sorry. "That's not fair."

Probably not, but she was weakening and that couldn't happen.

"No one ever said life would be fair, Dr. Steele—"

"Nathan. Remember?"

She was trying not to. "Didn't your mother ever tell you that?"

"She wasn't around much for heart-to-heart chats. I pretty much figured that one out on my own, though." An edgy tone crept into his voice. "Look, Cindy, I said I was sorry—"

"No. You really didn't. I heard the word apology and a detailed justification for why you went off on me for no good reason. Not once, though, did I hear you say the word *sorry*."

"Well, I am." He saw her look and added, "Sorry, that is. I was wrong."

"Wow, the world has gone mad. The *w* word actually passed your lips. As I live and breathe." Her skin started to tingle when she mentioned his lips and it didn't help that he kept staring at her. "I'll be sure not to spread that around. Who'd believe me anyway?"

"While we're setting the record straight, I feel it's only fair to point out that you were wrong, too."

"About what?" Her whole life consisted of being wrong one too many times, so a clarification was necessary.

"Me," he said. "I'll admit sometimes I can be a jerk at work. After all we've established that I did chastise you unjustly. But I take exception to the reputation remark. Mine is impeccable. And I'm not inflexible."

"Okay, then. Color me corrected."

"I'm not finished."

"Right. What else have you got?"

"People *do* like me."

By *people* she was pretty sure he meant women. It would be far too easy to be one of them and that simply couldn't happen. She was too close to getting what she'd worked so hard for. There was light at the end of a long, dark financial and educational tunnel and she couldn't afford *not* to focus on either of those fronts now.

Eyes straight ahead. No distractions; no detours.

"There's probably some truth to that," she agreed. "Someone undoubtedly does like you. File it under 'good to know.' Now, I've got work to do—"

"As do I. It's time to check on Rocky."

"Who?"

"The little guy. From yesterday. How could you possibly forget when you took one for the team?"

"Is that what you call it?"

"My story and I'm sticking to it." He smiled, and the power of it was awesome. "It's what the nurses call him. Somehow the nicknames just seem to stick."

"Rocky. A fighter." That tugged at her heart big time and she needed her space, stat, before she bought into him being a bona fide hero even after yesterday when he'd made her feel like the lowest of the low. He fought for the most defenseless and delicate of God's creatures. How long could she sustain this weak, borderline unjustifiable case of self-righteous indignation? How did she protect herself from him?

"Okay, then," she said, starting to turn away. His hand on her arm froze the movement. She could feel the warmth of his fingers and it had nothing to do with the protective suit keeping in body heat.

"Wait. There's one more thing."

There always was. How many ways did she not need this in her life? She forced herself to meet his gaze and braced to repel the reaction. "What?"

"Your phone number."

"What about it?" That was a stall. By definition one needed a number to dial to contact someone else on a telephone.

What she didn't know was *why* he wanted hers. Surely he didn't really want to call *her*. She'd admit to having the tiniest little crush on him after last night. Sleep had finally come when she'd realized that it wasn't really something to worry about because they were on completely different rungs of the hospital social ladder. But now he knew exactly who she was and had brought up the subject again. What was up with that?

"I'm asking for your phone number," he patiently explained.

"I don't give out that information," she said.

"Why?"

"Why do you want it?"

Now he rolled his eyes. "I'd like to call you sometime."

"So you can yell at me after hours, too?"

"Of course not." His gaze narrowed. "Has anyone ever talked to you about this acute flair you have for the dramatic? *And* holding a grudge?"

"Not recently."

"Look, I'd like your number so I can ask—"

"Don't say it."

He moved in a completely different orbit and she existed in the real world. Under normal circumstances there wasn't a chance in hell that their worlds would collide, but that changed last night and an alternate reality was initiated.

Now he was trying to change the order of the universe. When the last man in her life cleaned out her savings and maxed out her existing credit cards and ones he took out in her name, she learned the hard lesson that men have ulterior motives. The only unknown was how much it would cost her. She absolutely would not be a victim of whatever it was that Nathan Steele was planning.

"Why shouldn't I say it?" There was a charming, confident look on his face.

"Because yesterday you only made me *feel* like an idiot. If I gave you my number now, that would make it true."

She walked into the NICU before he could respond. There was nothing left to do except work through the bittersweet, wistful feeling inside that made her wish a man hadn't screwed up her life. Then she might be tempted to take a chance that another man wasn't going to do the same thing.

Nathan wasn't sure why he cruised the cafeteria at lunchtime instead of going to the doctor's dining room. Then he saw Cindy Elliott sitting by herself and the motivation for his detour became clear. It was an excuse to talk to her. Damage control for his unreasonable behavior, he told himself. But *himself* wasn't quite buying into that story. After her over-the-top reaction to his apology for unreasonable behavior, he'd turned over the unreasonable behavior crown to her. Yet he couldn't stop his own curiosity at her response.

He grabbed a tray and stepped into line, then picked up a ready-made turkey sandwich and a bottle of water. After paying for the items, he looked around, half-expecting her to be gone. She had a way of running out on him. This time she was still sitting alone at a table for two by the wall. Convenient.

"Here goes nothing," he mumbled to himself.

Sunshine leaked through the windows from the hospital's dome tower above this room, allowing the light in. The hum of voices buzzed around him. Balancing the rectangular green tray, he snaked his way through the Formica-topped tables and metal chairs with orange plastic seats.

He stopped beside her and did a replay of what he'd asked last night. "Is this seat taken?"

Her eyes narrowed on him when she looked up. "What if I said I was expecting someone?"

"Are you?"

"No."

Without waiting for permission, he set down his tray and sat in the chair opposite her. He sort of missed the "bunny suit." Now she was wearing the work uniform of cotton pants and dark-blue scrubs top with *Environmental Services* embroidered on the breast. In this light, her eyes were even more interesting—darker brown with flecks of gold. Definitely cinnamon. Spicy. Interesting. Not unlike the lady herself.

"So, how's it going?" He unwrapped the plastic on his sandwich and took a bite.

"Until now there was only one black mark on the day. In the last five seconds that just doubled." She set her spoon down. "Why are you here?"

"I'm hungry?"

"You know that's not what I meant. You could be having lobster, caviar and truffles in the doctor's dining room."

"Actually I think it's pheasant under glass and baked Alaska day. I'm not a big fan of either," he said.

"Again, not my point. You're here with the peasants. Why is that?"

"Maybe I find the environment here more interesting." He finished the first half of his sandwich and glanced at her empty bowl with wrappers piled up in it. "Soup and crackers isn't much for lunch."

"I'm on a diet."

"Why?" Nathan twisted the top off his water bottle and took a drink.

"By definition diet implies trying to drop a few pounds." Her tone was conversational, but mistrust lurked in her eyes.

"Again I ask—why?" He wagged a warning finger when she opened her mouth to answer. "Don't give me the snarky, sarcastic response that I know is on the tip of your tongue. You're not overweight."

"Why else would I go on a diet?" She leaned back and folded her arms over her chest. The classic stubborn, you're-not-getting-anything-out-of-me pose.

"All well and good for someone who needs to shape up, but you don't."

"How do you know?"

"Because I saw you in that dress last night."

The sexy, sensuous image would be imprinted on his mind forever. And he'd held her in his arms. She had curves in all the right places and not one of those places needed to slim down. The memory of her body pressed against his sent a flood of testosterone surging through him. And it wasn't the first time he'd reacted to her that way.

"Why are you really eating this?" he asked.

"Why do you care?"

"Good question. Humor me."

"Would you believe I have irritable bowel syndrome and this is a bland diet?"

"No."

She was irritable, but that wasn't a medical diagnosis.

It had something to do with him personally. Just a feeling, but he was pretty sure this snappish attitude had a lot to do with him not recognizing her, especially after coming down on her for something she hadn't done. And since his apology hadn't produced any discernible softening in her, that cranked up his curiosity.

"Okay." She tapped her lip thoughtfully. "What if I'm still full from last night?"

"Doubtful. You didn't finish the rubber chicken or even touch the prefab cheesecake." He would know. He'd noticed that, along with everything else about her. She was quick-witted, smart and sexy. A triple threat.

She sipped from the straw in her iced tea, then asked, "Are you going to let this go any time soon?"

"That's not my current plan, no."

She sighed. "If you must know, I'm always on a very tight budget the week before payday. Something you probably have no frame of reference for."

"Budgets? Or payday?"

"Either. Both."

"I get the concept, but you're right. It's not something I had to deal with."

"Had?"

"I didn't have a childhood, but not because money was a problem."

He'd had his hands full coping with family issues. And thinking about that could put multiple black marks on his day. Cindy, however, could brighten up an entire room. He'd found that out last night. And she was much more interesting than memories of the clinically dysfunctional Steele family.

"So," he said, rolling the empty plastic from his sandwich into a ball. "The south of France with Mumsy isn't in the budget?"

Her mouth twitched. She wanted to laugh but was holding back. "About that—"

"No need to explain."

"In my small way, I was getting even with you for yelling at me."

"I get that. What's your excuse for being crabby now?" he asked. "Lack of sleep? Staying out too late last night?"

"You got me. Hobnobbing with the rich and famous wore me out. I stayed up way past my bedtime."

And speaking of beds, an image of her in his with twisted sheets tightened a knot of need inside him that had started fewer than twenty-four hours ago when he'd seen her walk like sex in motion across a crowded room. Talking with her, discovering her sharp mind and keen sense of humor had only intensified the feeling. Then she'd really piqued his curiosity by abruptly walking out after cutting short their dance.

"It seemed like you were having fun. Why did you leave the party?" he asked.

"It was time to go." Something in her eyes said that wasn't the whole truth. "Now I've got a question for you— why are you stalking me?"

"That's harsh," he teased. "Take last night—"

"You mean when you didn't have a clue who I was?"

"No offense," he said, "But last night you weren't wearing the NICU jumpsuit."

"It's a legitimate question, Doctor—"

"Nathan, remember?"

The look on her face said she remembered it all and wasn't happy that she did. "My point is that a physician rubbing elbows with the peons here at Mercy Medical Center just isn't deliberately done. So the stalking remark is not out of line."

"It is if I just want to get to know you. And I do. We work

in the same place and it's inevitable that our paths would cross. Which is the reason I'd like your phone number."

"I don't really get the connection." She stood and picked up her tray. Over her shoulder as she was walking away, she said, "And you should just let it go, *Doctor.*"

Nathan knew she was right. He should let it go.

He honestly didn't understand why he couldn't. The average woman would be happy to go out with him. Clearly Cindy wasn't average, which could explain part of her appeal. The other part was curiosity. She wouldn't even give him a chance, and he was pretty sure that wasn't about him chastising her.

Cindy Elliott was quite the mystery and he wasn't finished trying to solve her. He'd see her stubborn and raise her a healthy dose of persistence.

Chapter Three

Cindy had clocked in from lunch after her unexpected encounter with Nathan and was now back to work. The afternoon stop in the NICU was next on her work sheet. Other than Dr. Charming going out of his way to talk to her in the cafeteria, it promised to be an ordinary afternoon. Then everything changed. And it all happened so fast.

One minute Cindy was running a long-handled dusting tool over the linoleum floor, the next Nathan was there with a tiny baby. He was calmly issuing orders like a general in the thick of battle.

The common sense move was to get out of the way even if directions to do just that in the event of a medical crisis hadn't been drilled into her. Cindy had been employed at Mercy Medical Center for nearly two years and had seen her share of medical situations but never one involving Nathan Steele. She knew what he did, had seen his medical practice partner in action, but she had never actually witnessed him saving a little life. And she had a bad feeling that her life was about to change. She couldn't help thinking that darn raffle ticket had somehow altered fate to put her in his orbit.

From her protected position against the wall she could hear the team talking and knew the baby boy was a twenty-five-weeker born just minutes ago by C-section. That made him about four months premature. He was already intubated, and they were using a bag to force air into his lungs. The person bagging the baby was her friend, Harlow Marcelli, who worked in the Respiratory Therapy department.

Cindy couldn't really see what the staff was doing to the baby, but Nathan was taller than everyone and the strain and intensity on his face were clearly visible. When bodies parted, she noticed that he was using two fingers on the tiny chest, compressions for cardiopulmonary resuscitation.

After listening with the stethoscope, he said, "Let's get him on a ventilator. IV line stat and electrodes for EKG. I need to surf him."

She made a mental note to ask what that meant.

Meanwhile, the troops moved to follow his orders, and moments later there were tubes and machines in place. Tracings on the monitors were blue, green and pink—each to distinguish a different function to be watched.

"I need blood gases," Nathan said.

Instantly Harlow moved, like a runner off the block at the sound of the starting pistol. In a few minutes, Nathan looked at the readings and nodded.

"He's a fighter. I think the little gladiator is stable for the moment. Watch him. I want to know if anything changes. I'll be right outside." He looked at the staff who'd fought with him. "Great job, everyone. I'm going to talk to the dad. Mom's still in recovery."

Cindy moved slightly to her right, to see through the double glass doors and out into the hall. The father was probably in his late twenties or early thirties, blonde and blue eyed, with terror all over his face. She couldn't hear what was said, but as Nathan talked some of the fear drained from the man's expression, leaving your garden-variety worry in its wake. When the man glanced over, she could also see love for the tiny little life fighting to survive. The gladiator, Nathan had called him.

Just last night he'd told her that if he couldn't see or touch something, he didn't believe it existed. How could he not see the love in that father's eyes?

"He's pretty awesome, isn't he?"

Cindy jumped at the sound of her friend's voice, then turned. "You startled me. I didn't know you were there."

"Yeah. I can see you're distracted." Harlow Marcelli was a pretty, green-eyed brunette and the fairy godmother who'd loaned her the patched-up pumps for the fundraiser.

"Not preoccupied. Just doing my job," she defended.

"Yeah." Her friend glanced to where the two men were still talking. "If your job is to watch Dr. Hot Stuff."

"Not my day to keep an eye on him." Cindy deliberately turned her back to the doors. "No matter how many times I see you do your thing, it never fails to amaze me. You were pretty awesome just now."

"Thanks." Harlow slid a glance over her shoulder at the isolette surrounded by state-of-the-art equipment. "He's not out of the woods yet. I hope he's a fighter like the doc said."

"Me, too. The gladiator." She smiled.

"The staff usually gives the preemies nicknames," Harlow explained, echoing what Nathan had already told her. "Something inspirational to live up to."

"Live being the operative word. It surprised me coming

from Nathan—" She stopped when the other woman gave her a funny look.

"Since when do you call him by his first name?"

"Oh, that—"

"Yeah, that."

Cindy glanced over her shoulder where he still stood in the hall. "We sat at the same table at the fundraiser last night."

"And?"

"The glue on your shoe didn't hold up."

"Later with the shoes news." Harlow's green eyes snapped with impatience. "When did you start calling Dr. Charming *Nathan?*"

"Last night. When he asked me to."

"Why?" Her friend added, "Did he ask you to, I mean?"

"Probably because he didn't know who I was."

"I need more information than that."

Cindy gripped the long handle of her dusting device. "He sat next to me, bought me a drink and said I looked familiar, but he couldn't place me."

"He didn't recognize you?" Surprise jumped into Harlow's eyes.

"Not even when I made him guess."

"You didn't," her friend scoffed.

"I did." Cindy had her reasons and it had seemed like a good idea at the time.

"Hot damn," Harlow said. "I can't wait to tell Whitney and Mary Frances that we literally transformed you into a mystery woman. That's so cool."

"Not really. When I saw him this morning, he figured it out."

When he smelled her perfume. That memory made her stomach do a funny little shimmy and she told herself it was only because something that sensitive was out of character for Nathan Steele.

"Was he mad?"

It would have been easier if he had been. Then giving him a hard time would have been justified and not just turned her into a roaring witch.

"No. He took it well. Even apologized to me for over-reacting and yelling at me in here yesterday. Then he asked for my phone number again," Cindy explained.

The other woman's jaw dropped. "Again?"

"I refused to give it to him when he asked me last night. After he caught up with me. And he only did because your shoe broke."

"He chased you?" Harlow folded her arms over her chest. "This gets better and better."

"It was time for me to go."

"Apparently he didn't agree."

"That's just because my identity was still in question and that intrigued him," Cindy said. "Sort of like when a superhero assumes an alter ego. It's the whole don't-I-know-her-from-somewhere? thing."

"Then what was his excuse for asking again today?"

"He's one of those guys who can't take no for an answer."

"And why should he? Women in this hospital are taking numbers in the line to snap him up." Warning slid into her friend's eyes. "Let him call. You don't have to commit to anything. And I wouldn't if I were you."

"Preaching to the choir, H," Cindy said. "I don't have time for the games."

Just then Nathan walked back into the unit to check on the baby.

"Gotta go," Harlow said.

Cindy turned away and finished her job in the NICU,

then slipped out the door. Her clean cart was against the wall in the hall. She was still putting away her cleaning supplies when she heard the doors behind her whisper open. It could have been anyone, but not just anyone made the hair at her nape prickle. Only Nathan did that and the development was recent. And, annoyingly enough, recurring.

"Cindy—"

She turned around. "Did I forget to do something in the unit?"

"No. I just—" He ran his fingers through his hair. "I saw you talking to Harlow."

"She's my friend. One of the fairy godmothers, actually."

"Good to know her talents are more than just being one of the best respiratory techs here at Mercy Medical."

"Speaking of that," she said. "I was watching just now, when you were working on the gladiator."

"Don't ask me where that came from," he said sheepishly. The look was too darn cute.

"Okay. But I wanted to ask something else." Anything to take the edge off his appeal. She met his gaze and said, "What did you mean when you said 'surf' him?"

"Surfactin. It's a medication."

"Yeah. I was pretty sure you weren't talking about ocean waves. What does it do?"

"Makes the lungs more flexible. If they're stiff, air can't be pushed in and out," he explained. "One of the problems in neonates is that their lungs are immature. The medication helps them function better until they fully develop."

"I see."

"Good. Now I've got one for you."

"One what?"

"Question. Turnabout is fair play." He leaned a broad shoulder against the wall.

If the inquiry was about how a guy could look so sexy dressed in utilitarian scrubs, she had no answer. On every possible level it was just wrong for him to be so yummy in shapeless cotton material with a drawstring at the waist of the pants. The V-neck shirt at least revealed the hint of chest hair, but really, the ensemble left a lot to be desired. Except the guy in it was more desirable than her favorite chocolate with caramel.

"Okay. You can ask," she said, knowing she was really going to regret giving permission.

"What do you have against giving me your phone number?" he said.

"You'll use it," she answered. "Gotta get back to work now."

She grabbed her cart and pushed it down the hall, feeling his gaze lasering into her back until she rounded the corner. Leaning against the wall, she blew out a long breath.

It was hard work going one on one with a hero. Even harder to remember why she needed to not get sucked into the games. Between work and school, she didn't have the time or energy. Whatever he was selling, she wasn't buying. And even if she were, she'd just blown any chance with him. Like Harlow said, women were waiting in line.

So much for her plan to attend the fundraiser and enjoy every moment. Pulling out those memories of how the beautiful people lived was supposed to brighten her daily grind. She'd made memories, all right, and so much more. She'd snagged the doctor's attention. For all the good that would do.

After today he wouldn't waste any more time on her. Which was just as well because she didn't have the time, energy or emotional reserves to waste on him.

And that made her sad and angry. It made her wish that once upon a time, she hadn't been duped and damaged by a dope.

As Nathan headed down the hall toward administration, he was mentally fine-tuning his case to hire extra staff for the NICU. For the past week things had been nuts. Gladiator, aka Dylan Mason, was the first of some really sick babies. The staff in the unit was working their asses off and he wanted more bodies to care for his patients. Still, it wouldn't be easy to convince the powers-that-be to spend more money, and he braced for the coming battle.

But when he walked into the outer office and saw Cindy at the desk, battles of the sexy sort took center stage. Probably because she'd refused every request to let him call her.

He'd never worked that hard for a phone number and, frankly, the struggle made him even more determined to get to the bottom of her resistance.

Cindy watched warily as he moved closer then settled his hip on the corner of her desk. There were two metal-framed chairs in front of it, but invading her space was more appealing. And this place could use a healthy dose of interesting. The ocean scenes on the beige walls made it generic decorating. With her blond hair and warm brown eyes, she sure brightened up her surroundings.

"Is there any job in this hospital that you don't do?" he asked.

"Brain surgery."

He laughed and that hadn't been his expectation on his way to the administration offices. "So, can I ask what you're doing here?"

"You can *ask*." The way her full mouth curved up in a

teasing smile finished the implication that she didn't have to answer. "I'm an administrative intern."

"Right. I remember. In addition to your other job?"

She nodded. "After the fall semester, I'll have my degree in hospital administration. This summer was a good time to get the internship part accomplished."

"Busy girl."

She shrugged and the movement did amazing things to her breasts under the pink, silky blouse. By peeking over the desk he could see her black slacks. The business attire was buttoned-down professional. He'd also seen her in plain housekeeping clothes. But by far his favorite look was that short, strapless dress he'd first seen her in. The memory caused a very physical reaction that was a good indication his desire to see her out of it hadn't gone away.

"So," she said, tapping her pen on the desk. "I'm going to take a wild guess that you're here to see Mr. Ryan. And not stalking me."

"You would be correct. I have a staffing issue to discuss with him."

"Specifically?"

"There's a lot of work in the NICU. We're going nuts up there."

"And you want more help," she guessed.

"Right in one."

She swiveled her chair to the right and faced the computer monitor, then clicked away on the keyboard until data scrolled onto the screen. After studying it for a moment, she turned back and looked up.

"Good luck with that."

He stared at her for several moments, then said, "What?"

"I'm pretty sure Mr. Ryan won't give his approval to hire any more people."

"You can tell that by looking at the computer?"

"Yes."

He stood and looked down. "What is it? The great and powerful Oz?"

She grinned. "Pay no attention to the man behind the curtain."

"Seriously? How can a computer tell you we're not up to our necks in alligators?"

"All the productivity information is here. It's about FTEs—"

"No acronyms, please."

"Full time equivalents. Then there are RVUs—" She noticed his frown and her full mouth curved up. "Relative value units."

"Dumb it down for me."

He knew matching personnel to patient load was complicated but had deliberately steered clear of the minutiae because it wasn't his problem. Now avoidance was paying off because she was talking to him.

"There's a formula to determine the percentage of staff hours per patient day for every hospital department. For example, if you're allowed four hours to get the job done and do it in three hours and forty-five minutes, you're over a hundred percent. That's exactly where administration wants it and you're the best thing since sliced bread."

"What if I want two more nurses?"

She turned to the computer, clicked the keys and assimilated the information that popped up. "According to this, NICU productivity is at ninety-four percent."

"That sounds pretty good."

"Not really. It means you have to give up a nurse."

"You're kidding," he said.

"Do I look like I'm kidding?"

No, but she looked like she was enjoying this more than

was absolutely necessary. She also looked like a woman who needed a full-body-contact kiss and he was just the relative value unit to give it to her.

"So, what happens if the NICU is full and the perinatologist sends over a high-risk pregnancy patient who delivers a twenty-four-week baby? How do I get a nurse?"

"The percentages are set at safe staffing levels. But in an extreme case, you contact the on-call nurse. If there's a need for more help, you try to catch someone else at home and ask them to come in."

"And what if we can't find someone?"

"What if a brontosaurus walks in with two eggs and one of them cracks?" She folded her hands on the desk.

He knew what she was getting at, but this spirited back and forth was the most fun he'd had since the last time they'd talked.

"And your point is?" he asked, settling into the chair in front of her desk for a full-on view of her.

"You can't staff for 'what if.' In a perfect world, yes. But we go by averages, then adjust to the reality we're dealing with."

"When I go in to see Ryan, am I going to get a rewind and play of this whole conversation?" It had been much more palatable coming from her, he realized.

"Probably."

"Well, I'm already here." And so was she. He had the testosterone rush to prove it. "Might as well go in and try to grind him down."

"Good luck."

Speaking of luck... It was time to stop talking shop and try again to grind *her* down. Or at least find out what her beef was with him.

"I'm having a NICU meeting today at five o'clock.

Nurses, respiratory therapy. You should come. Everyone who works in the unit is invited."

"I don't work there." Pink crept into her cheeks. "At least not on the babies."

"Consider this part of your administrative internship. Good experience to come and hear the opposing point of view."

"As tempting as that is…"

That was a no without saying *no*. And he knew she really didn't need to be there. Personnel and administration were like Democrats and Republicans. They'd never see eye to eye. He just wanted the opportunity to spend a little time with her.

"I'd really like to see you." He wasn't talking about the meeting, and the way her eyes narrowed told him she knew it. "But this is me *not* using your phone number."

"Look, Nathan, I'm really flattered that you asked. Partly because I thought that ship had sailed last week. But mostly because…" She stopped, clearly weighing how much to say. "Because every single woman younger than fifty who works in this facility, and some who don't, are waiting in line to give you their phone numbers. But I'm not one of them."

"Why is that?"

"Mostly because I can't help wondering why you keep asking."

"You mean am I up to something?" he asked.

"I mean is it just stubbornness? Ego? You being contrary?"

"Is it so hard to believe that I want to get to know you better?"

"Oh, please." She made a scoffing sound. "That's code for hooking up."

He wouldn't say no to a hookup, but that wasn't his

primary objective. "I'd really like to see you outside of work."

"Let me be clear. And honest. You said it yourself. I'm a busy girl. I don't have time in my schedule for a fling."

"Neither do I."

Her eyes flashed with what looked like anger and frustration. "In my experience, guys like you are all about the one who said no."

"Later I'm probably going to be annoyed at being lumped in with the jerks."

She ignored that and continued. "Let's just skip to the end. How about if I just sleep with you? Then I can get you out of my life. It's not even necessary to buy me dinner. It will save us both time. Seven minutes tops."

"Ouch." He'd heard both heat and hurt in her voice, and that took the sting out of the words for him. If only it had canceled out his curiosity, but he wasn't that lucky. "What if I *want* to buy you dinner? No strings."

"Do you?" she asked suspiciously.

"Take a chance. Find out for yourself."

"If I do will you go away quietly?"

"Can we just take this one step at a time?" he asked. "Don't spoil the surprise. That takes all the fun out of it."

"In my experience, there's nothing fun about a surprise."

That was the second time she'd mentioned her experience. It didn't take a mental giant to figure out that whatever happened hadn't been good. If Nathan was as smart as everyone thought, he'd run from Cindy and her emotional baggage. But apparently he wasn't that bright. Because he was inclined to sit here and wait until she agreed to go out with him.

"You know you want to say yes," he coaxed.

"Were you raised by wolves? What part of *no* do you not understand?" She glared at him.

"My parents were incredibly civilized. Just not to each other." He refused to take the bait. It didn't escape his notice that she was pulling out all the stops to get him to give up. That made the challenge of wearing her down all the more stimulating. "Come on, Cindy. It will be fun."

"The *Titanic* was fun, too, if you like freezing cold water and gigantic icebergs opening up the side of your ship like a tuna can."

"I'm not leaving until you agree to have dinner with me tonight." Tonight because he didn't want to give her time to back out.

She thought for several moments and apparently decided he wasn't backing down. After an exaggerated sigh, she said, "All right. But only because I have to eat."

"I'll pick you up at seven."

Chapter Four

Cindy peeked out the window of her tiny three-bedroom home in the old part of Henderson. Nathan wasn't there yet, but it was only six-fifty. She still had ten minutes to fret over and change the sleeveless black cotton sundress that had been her second outfit choice. If only her fairy godmothers were here with borrowed clothes, shoes and much-needed advice because she was running low on clothing options and was fresh out of common sense. A limited budget didn't allow for a large wardrobe. Lack of variety sure cut down on time spent making a decision, but that didn't erase the desperate wish to not care so much about looking her very best.

Because impressing Nathan Steele wasn't the goal for tonight. Men were trouble and she didn't need any more of it. This dinner was all about getting the doctor to back off and leave her alone so she could focus on her internship and the current job that helped pay her mountain of bills.

Cindy paced the living room's wood floor and stayed far away from a mirror that would send her fashion critique impulses into warp drive. The back-and-forth walking lasted for another five minutes before she lifted the edge of the dollar store criss-crossed lace curtains just as a small, sporty silver Mercedes pulled up to the curb. The nerves she'd barely kept under control did a synchronized freak out.

"This is a very bad idea," she muttered.

She grabbed the lightweight black sweater and her purse from the cedar chest that doubled as a coffee table sitting in front of the green floral love seat. Then she waited by the door for his knock. When it came, she whispered one Mississippi, two Mississippi, and continued until she got to ten before opening the door and forcing a bright smile.

"Hi. You're early."

Nathan's gaze slid from the top of her head to her red-painted toes and the casual black and white low-heeled sandals. There was a gleam in his eyes when he smiled. "The rumor is that you're on a tight schedule so wasting time wasn't an option. And you're obviously ready. You look beautiful."

"Thanks."

It was just a line, she told herself. He was only being polite. But all the disclaimers in the world couldn't stop the glow that went nuclear inside her and the tightness in her chest when she looked at him. The sexy scruff on his cheeks and jaw was missing, proof that he'd shaved. For her.

That started more flutters in her stomach, but she managed to say, "You're not so bad yourself."

The truth was that he didn't have a bad look. She'd seen him in scrubs and in a tux. The current crisply pressed khaki slacks and cream-colored sport shirt showed off the tan on his muscular arms with the added benefit of enhancing his broad shoulders and trim waist. It was impossible to pick a favorite Nathan view when he looked like sin-for-the-taking in everything.

Or nothing?

That thought sent hormones surging through her, and she quickly stepped outside on the porch. After locking the door she said, "Let's go."

Nathan followed behind her on the sidewalk so if he found her hurried exit weird, she didn't know, what with not being able to see his expression. At the curb he opened the car, then cupped her elbow in his palm, handing her inside. The touch did nothing to calm her nerves. In fact it started tingles line dancing up and down her arms.

Before there was time to anesthetize them, he was in the driver's seat, starting the car. The interior was small and intimate, not nearly enough space to dissipate the masculine scent of his skin. It surrounded her as surely as if he held her in his arms. Less than two weeks ago he'd done just that, the night he hadn't recognized her. Being that close to him had stirred a fair amount of panic and then she'd made a dash for the exit.

He'd only caught up with her because her shoe broke. Moments later she'd called him a jerk and he'd laughed, then said he wanted to see her again. Turning him down flat hadn't worked so well and here she was, out of the frying pan and into the fire. So to speak.

Speaking of speaking, she wasn't doing any, so she tried to think of something witty to say. All she could come up with was, "So where are you taking me?"

Before turning left onto Lake Mead Boulevard, he glanced over. "Have you ever had a nice surprise?"

She wasn't sure why he'd asked but gave the question

some serious thought. "Probably, but I can't remember one off the top of my head."

"Well, brace yourself. I promise this one will be good."

He turned from Horizon Ridge Parkway onto Eastern Avenue and drove up the hill, then pulled into the parking lot of Capriotti's Italian restaurant. It was dusk and not the optimum time to appreciate the lights across the Vegas Valley, but after the sun set, there would be a spectacular view.

Inside, the muted light made for a romantic atmosphere, and a cozy booth for two in the back corner cranked it up several notches. Their arms touched and Cindy swore she actually heard the crackle of electricity that was anything but static. A little sideways move gave her space but no real breathing room.

The last time a guy had taken her to a restaurant with candles and white tablecloths, he'd sweet-talked his way into her life and her bank account, then proceeded to rob her blind. Nathan probably didn't need her money, but he stirred a need deep inside and she had an uneasy feeling that he could take from her something far more precious than her good credit rating.

A forty-something waiter with salt-and-pepper hair and wearing black pants and a long-sleeved white shirt appeared beside them. "Dr. Steele, it's nice to see you again."

Nathan's smile was friendly. "Hello, Mario. How are you?"

"Very well." He looked at Cindy and bowed slightly. "Welcome to Capriotti's. May I get you something from the bar?"

Dr. Charming met her gaze. "What would you like?"

"Surprise me," she said wryly.

"Mario, I think we'll have a bottle of my favorite wine."

"The pinot noir. Excellent choice. I'll bring it right out." Before leaving, he handed them menus.

When they were alone Cindy opened hers and said, "So they know your favorite wine. Obviously, you come here often."

"The food is really good."

"Do your other women like it?" She was looking at the food choices but not really seeing the words. When she glanced up she saw that he looked more amused than anything else.

"My other women?" he asked. "In spite of what you think and the hospital gossip you base it on, there is no line of women."

Before she could refute that, someone delivered a basket containing warm rolls wrapped in a white cloth. With a flourish, the guy mixed oil and balsamic vinegar on a plate for dipping. Then Mario returned with the bottle of red and skillfully opened it with a corkscrew and twist of the wrist. After Nathan sipped and approved, the waiter poured them each a glass.

"Do you need a moment or are you ready to order?"

"Cindy?"

She saw fettuccine alfredo and pointed, "I'll have that."

"My favorite," Nathan agreed. "Make it two. And two Caesar salads."

"Excellent choice," Mario approved, then quietly left them.

Nathan picked up his wineglass. "Here's to good surprises."

"From your mouth to God's ear." There was a crystal

ring when she touched her glass to his. After taking a drink she said, "That's very nice."

"See? Already something good." He grinned.

She wasn't so sure. The night wasn't over yet and getting through unscathed was a goal in jeopardy when he looked at her like she was dessert. That wouldn't be a problem except she *wanted* to be dessert.

He leaned back against the leather seat and stretched an arm along the back, his fingers nearly brushing her bare shoulder. "So, how are mumsy and daddy?"

"Actually my parents both passed away several years ago. My father nursed mom through cancer. Then a couple of years later, he had a heart attack."

"I'm sorry, Cindy. I didn't mean to bring up—it was a bad joke."

"My fault. I was messing with you that night at the fundraiser." She settled her white cloth napkin in her lap. "It was hard losing them both so close together, but Dad was never the same after Mom died. I think he missed her. Now it's just my brother and me."

"Is he coming home from college for the summer?"

"No. He's taking a class, working and sharing an apartment with some buddies. I'm helping out with expenses." Which wouldn't be necessary if the sweet-talking jerk who'd wined and dined her hadn't cleaned out the money her parents left for their children's education. She took a sip of wine. "You already know about my pathetically normal childhood. I'd like to hear about how you didn't have one."

He frowned, an expression just this side of brooding but no less appealing than his grin. "My father was always working. Because he was never home, Mother had hobbies. She took classes. Painting. Knitting. Needlepoint. Calligraphy. Aura reading." Over the flickering light of the candle, his gaze connected with hers. "Neither of them were around much. I became pretty self-sufficient."

"It sounds to me like your mother was hurt about your father working so much. She was probably hiding in her hobbies." She finished off the wine in her glass. "And I can't decide if you take after her or your father."

"How about neither?"

She shook her head. "You put in a lot of hours at the hospital."

"And you know this—how?"

"While the women wait in your line, they talk about you." The snarky remark made him smile, just as she'd intended. "It's said that you're dedicated. So either you're a workaholic like your father, or you're hiding like your mom."

Just then Mario brought their salads. "Is there anything else I can get you?"

"Not right now," Nathan said.

The light, carefree expression had disappeared and it was her fault. Cindy wished for a filter from her brain to her mouth, but it was too late for that.

They ate in silence for a few minutes. At least he did. She pushed romaine lettuce and croutons around the plate and not much of it got eaten. She wished she'd kept her views to herself.

Finally she couldn't stand the silence. "Look, Nathan, it's just my opinion and worth what you paid for it. About now you're probably regretting this invitation. The offer of sex with no strings attached must look pretty good. Sometimes I don't know when to keep my mouth shut."

His eyes turned even darker with an intensity that was almost tangible as his gaze settled on her mouth. "Let's just say you've given me food for thought. Perspective that's both sincere and sweet."

Yay her. It felt like he'd yelled at her even though he hadn't raised his voice. Unlike that day at the hospital, this time he had a reason to be mad. Amateur psychoanalysis probably wasn't what he'd signed up for tonight in his quest to know her. He'd no doubt learned everything necessary to form the opinion that this night had been a cheap validation for her pronouncement that he should have taken no for an answer.

Two hours later after more to eat and drink and entertaining, idle conversation, they were standing in front of her open door. Cindy was pleasantly full and still rocking a lovely buzz from his favorite red wine.

"Thanks for dinner." She looked up and her breath caught.

The inside light showed the glitter in Nathan's eyes as his knuckles lightly grazed her cheek. "I'm going to kiss you."

"Do you really think that's a good idea—"

"No. But all night I haven't been able to take my eyes off you. I want to see how that sexy, sassy, smart mouth tastes."

Her heart started to pound until she thought it would jump right out of her chest. "Oh, my—"

"I can't help it." He tucked a strand of hair behind her ear with a shaking hand. "I want to feel all the passion you put into being so tough."

Words were trapped in her throat so she started to shake her head. The feel of his lips stopped her as surely as it shut down all rational thought. One moment his mouth was on hers and the next she was plastered against his body, her arms twining around his neck. His big, warm hands restlessly rubbed up and down her back until her skin prickled with awareness and every nerve ending was on fire. Her breasts were crushed to his chest and ached for the touch of his hand.

In an awkward, erotic dance, he maneuvered her inside then closed the door. As he backed her against the wall, the sound of their raspy, ragged breathing filled her small front room and she let her purse fall off her shoulder. When her arms were around his neck again, he slid his palm over her hip then down her thigh before inching up the hem of her dress.

He hooked his finger into the waistband of her panties and drew them down until she stepped out of the restraining prim cotton. Kissing her senseless, he slipped a finger inside her and played until she was mindless with desire. A breathy moan escaped her throat and he groaned.

"Cindy," he breathed against her cheek. "I've wanted you since the night of that damned dinner. But if you don't want this, I'll—"

"No. I want…" Her voice was a wanton whisper. She'd never felt such a powerful need so completely consuming her. There was a very real possibility she would simply implode if he didn't take her in the next ten seconds. "Now. Nathan. Please. Do you have—"

"Yeah."

He dropped his wallet on the floor after pulling out a condom and lowered his pants and briefs before covering himself. Then he lifted her, and as her legs circled his waist, he entered her, bracing his forearm against the wall. The thickness of him filled her and took her breath away at the same time. He drove her higher and higher until she shattered into a thousand points of light and shuddered with the pieces of pleasure surging through her.

Moments later he went still and tightened his arms around her, groaning out his own release. As his breathing slowed, he buried his face in her neck and kissed her gently, tenderly. Finally he let her legs go and they slid down as he wrapped his strong arms around her waist and held her to him.

"Wow." He rested his forehead against hers. "There's no reason you should believe me, but I really didn't mean for that to happen."

"I know." And neither had she. For whatever reason, she believed him and here they were.

"Bathroom?" He was asking where it was. Hard to believe he hadn't been further inside than the front door.

"Down the hall," she said. "First door on the right."

When he was gone, she slipped her panties back on, picked up her purse and tried to figure out what to say when he returned.

It didn't take long. Unlike her with the nerves doing a rumba inside her, he looked as cool as Mount Charleston after the first winter snow. But the expression on his face told her there was a problem. And when had she learned to read him so well?

"What's wrong?" she asked.

"Probably nothing."

"Then why do you look like that?"

"The condom broke," he said.

She blinked at him, trying to make sense of what he was saying. "It broke?"

"That doesn't mean there's anything to worry about. It's probably fine," he assured her. "I just thought you should know even though the odds of pregnancy are slim."

And so it had been the perfect storm of an evening. Dinner. Sex. And a broken condom.

So what else was new? That was the story of her life.

Three weeks later the pregnancy odds went up when Cindy's normally punctual period was late. She'd told herself it could be delayed for any number of reasons and stress was at the top of her list. But just to cover her bases she'd peed on a stick and nearly fainted when the word *pregnant* appeared.

On an ironic note, in the twenty-one days since "seeing" Nathan, he hadn't once badgered her for a phone number or joined her in the cafeteria for lunch. So sleeping with him to get him out of her life had actually worked.

What she hadn't expected was relief and disappointment in equal parts. Then she did the pregnancy test and shock pushed out every other emotion.

She'd just gotten off work and was waiting in the hall outside the NICU for Nathan to be finished with hospital rounds. This wasn't the best place to talk, but she didn't know what else to do. Thanks to her, no phone numbers had been exchanged. And it seemed like forever before he came out of the unit, but that was probably normal when your life was falling apart.

Nathan stopped short when he saw her leaning against the far wall. There was an expression on his face that she couldn't decipher. And it didn't matter anyway.

"We need to talk." Her fingers twisted together as she looked to her left and right, making sure that employees moving in the hall were too far away to hear.

"Hello to you, too."

"Sorry. I'm a little freaked out."

"Ah. So we should go somewhere private?" he asked.

"That would probably be best."

He rubbed a hand across the back of his neck. "How about the Revello Lounge. It's at the M Resort. Do you know it?"

"I'll meet you there."

The one-year-old hotel was on the corner of Mercy Medical Center Parkway and Las Vegas Blvd. Fifteen minutes after leaving the hospital she turned left into the resort lot and found a parking place close to the lobby entrance. She walked inside and took the escalator up, stepping off onto the shiny marble floor. To her right was the gift shop, a café and a pastry place called Baby Cakes. Fate was having a laugh at her expense.

She found the lounge, which was all glass, amber lights and modern glitz. Nathan was waiting in a quiet corner and she took the leather barrel-backed chair across the chrome table from him. They each ordered club soda with lime. She would have preferred something stronger. There was no way to soften the news and she didn't try.

"I'm pregnant."

He was all brooding silence before saying, "I figured."

"I'm pretty sure when you promised me a good surprise at dinner you didn't mean a baby."

"I never planned for anything to happen."

She believed that, and yet he carried a condom. A faulty one.

Just then the cocktail waitress appeared with their drinks and set them down on napkins. "Can I get you anything else?"

Cindy figured she had about all she could stand and shook her head.

"We're good," Nathan said and the woman drifted away.

"You might be good, but I'm pregnant." Cindy picked up her drink and played with the straw. "This is Las Vegas and odds are fickle at best. But I can't believe my luck is this bad."

"Yours?" He was still in his scrubs and checked the pager on his waistband. "What about mine? It appears the planets aligned just right and you were fertile."

"Right back at you, buster," she said.

"I was hoping you were on an alternative method of birth control."

"Since I'm not seeing anyone, there was no reason." She glared at him. "And can we talk about the condom? That was yours so don't even try to make this my fault."

"That's not what I meant. Look, Cindy, I take full responsibility—"

"Don't." She couldn't handle an apology right now.

She'd been a willing participant as soon as his lips touched hers. For God's sake, she'd thought about him naked when he'd picked her up. All through dinner something had been sizzling between them. They'd had sex. Then nothing.

One minute he'd been pestering her for a phone number, the next he completely disappeared. Yet again she'd been fooled. He really was just one of those guys who refused to give up until he got what he wanted. This time he got more than he'd bargained for, but she was also paying a high price.

"This is not part of my plan," she said.

He nodded. "Plans have a way of changing."

Cindy felt a bubble of panic mix with hysteria that was barely held in check. She couldn't handle calm rationality any more than his apology. This was her life. She'd made a bad decision in the past but was working things out. For a short time there had been light at the end of the tunnel, and now it was connected to a speeding locomotive. All because she'd won that stupid raffle ticket and slid into hell when Nathan Steele noticed her.

"You don't understand," she said. "I have another semester of classes. I'm doing my internship, not to mention a full-time job. My bills aren't going to pay themselves.

And I'm putting my brother through college. Harry is my responsibility."

"It doesn't have to be all on you. He can get student loans."

"No. I can't let him do that. The subject of blame keeps coming up. Between you and me the fault for this pregnancy is about equal. But the fact that my brother's college money is gone is all on me." She put her glass back on the table without drinking any of the club soda in it. "I was supposed to take care of his college fund. My father left me in charge of the money. How can I tell him that what our father left for his education isn't there?

"My parents started putting away money for school when each of us was born. One of the last things Dad said to me was to see that my little brother graduated from UCLA. Harry wants to be a lawyer."

"Good for him."

"Not if he can't get his degree." Cindy twisted her fingers together in her lap.

"Why can't he?" Nathan's frown deepened. "What happened?"

"There was a guy." She met his gaze and figured he was thinking that there always was. "Conrad Worthington. At least that's what he said his name was. The cops couldn't find any trace of him."

"What did he do?"

"He charmed me into trusting him, told me he loved me, then cleaned out my bank account." She drew in a shuddering breath. "He maxed out my existing credit cards and all the ones he could get in my name."

"Son of a bitch." Nathan's hands, resting on the arms of the chair, curled into fists.

"Yeah. I called him that, too, and a few things I can't repeat. The banks refused to forgive the debt, but I managed to negotiate payments. I dropped out of school and worked two jobs for a while. When I had better control over the situation, I started taking a few night classes, which is why it's taking so long to get my degree. But I had everything under control and it was going according to plan. The thing is, I'm still paying for that mess. I can't afford another one." Even in the dim light she saw when his expression went from brooding to pity. She could stand just about anything but that. "And then you came along. Dr. Charming. Wanting my phone number and not taking no for an answer."

"I didn't mean for this to happen," he said again.

She believed him, but that didn't help when panic was her go-to emotion. "It's all fun and games until the condom breaks and someone gets pregnant."

Chapter Five

Nathan's head felt like it was ready to explode. It was a sensation that was becoming increasingly familiar where Cindy Elliott was concerned, but this time wasn't about passion. He struggled to process information that was a lot of fact swamped by buckets of emotion.

Fact: The condom broke.

Fact: She was pregnant.

Fact: The odds of this happening were ridiculously low, which put it firmly in the miracle column.

Emotion: He went from *holy crap my boys are badass* to *holy crap I'm going to be a father.*

That was a fact that gave him serious pause since he'd been parented in absentia and had no working model of how to raise a kid.

Cindy was staring at him, then abruptly she stood and slid her purse more firmly on her shoulder. "I just thought you should know about the baby."

"Are you leaving?" He didn't think she could surprise him any more, but somehow she always did.

"We're done here."

"Not by a long shot. Sit down."

"Why should I?"

He met her gaze and the fear there went a long way toward tamping down his irritation. "For one thing this habit you have of running out on me is really getting old."

"And?" She folded her arms over her chest. "You said 'for one thing,' which means there's another reason I should sit."

"We're not even close to being done here."

"What else is there to say?" Her tone oozed suspicion and mistrust, but she sat.

"I'm not sure," he admitted. "This is a shock."

"Tell me about it. At least you told me when—you know." She looked down, suddenly shy. Charmingly so.

Nathan knew she meant he'd warned her about the condom malfunction. He realized something else, too. She didn't trust him to not run out on her like the last bozo who'd robbed her blind then dumped on her and disappeared. If nothing else, being on his own as a kid had taught him to be the soul of responsibility.

He leaned toward her and rested his elbows on his knees as their gazes locked. Her brown eyes were a mixture of gold and cinnamon with a healthy dose of innocence thrown in. The vulnerability there tugged at him, making him want to fold her in his arms, a feeling that came out of nowhere. The things he couldn't explain made him acutely uncomfortable.

"Look, Cindy, you're not in this alone."

"What does that mean?" she asked.

"That we're in this together." How lame was that answer? he thought.

"Oh, so you're going to carry this baby for nine months?"

He hadn't realized doubts about her intentions to do just that were even in his mind until her sarcastic statement indicated otherwise. Relief coursed through him.

"The differences in our anatomy being what they are, I can't really do that—"

"But you would if you could," she finished wryly. "It's easy to promise something when there's no way you can possibly be held accountable for not following through."

Again he felt like he was paying the price for another guy's sin. "I'm not running out on you like the last son of a bitch."

Her gaze jumped to his as anger and hurt gleamed in her eyes. "So you'll be around."

"Yes."

"I see." Primly she folded her hands in her lap. "We already established that you can't take over getting big as a battleship or deal with enough water retention to float it. So what else is there?"

"We'll work it out as we go along," he offered.

"Maybe you could finish up my classes and the internship I need for my degree." She snapped her fingers and shook her head. "Nope. Wrong again. Someone would notice and I'd be out on my backside because of cheating."

"Look, Cindy—"

"Actually, I can probably finish all of that before the baby is born." She tapped her lip thoughtfully, but there was panic around the edges. "Then all I have to do is give birth and find a better job because I have to afford good child care along with having an infant who's depending on me. Piece of cake."

"The martyr act is admirable, but you didn't get like this on your own. I'll help you."

"So in between saving premature babies you're going to watch ours so I can finally get my career on track?"

"Like I said, we'll figure things out."

"I've never experienced a 'we.' There's always just been me. My body, my problem."

"My baby, too," he said quietly.

All the fight drained out of her and she leaned back in the club chair. "Just so you know, *I* know I'm being unreasonable. If it's all right with you, I think I'll blame it on pregnancy hormones."

"That works for me."

As a corner of her full mouth quirked up, he felt an absurd surge of desire. The subdued lighting here in the bar made a sexy shadow of the small dent in her chin and he desperately wanted to explore it with his tongue. Somehow during that brief, passionate encounter when they'd made a baby, he'd missed out on discovering every single inch of her and wanted another opportunity. Not likely now. A good thing because it wasn't rational. And definitely not smart.

He excelled at rational and smart, but somehow Cindy changed the rules on him. She was pregnant with his child and this was uncharted territory. It was also a medical condition and that was someplace to start.

He took a sip of his club soda. "Other than hormones, how are you feeling?"

"A little queasy," she admitted.

He wanted to say something clinically clever, tell her how to fix it, but this wasn't his specialty. "Have you seen an obstetrician?"

Her expression turned wry. "I just barely peed on the stick."

"So that would be a no," he concluded.

"No," she agreed.

"Okay." He nodded thoughtfully. "I can give you a couple of names. But Rebecca Hamilton is at the top of the list. She's very good and I think you'd be comfortable with her."

"I'll see if she's a tier-one doctor on the Mercy Medical insurance plan."

"I'm sure she is because she has medical privileges there. If not, I'll take care of it."

"It? What does that mean?" Tension made her straighten in the club chair.

"I'll take care of the expenses."

"Because?"

"It's my responsibility."

Her eyes narrowed. "Wow, that gave me a warm and fuzzy feeling."

"Is that the hormones talking again?"

"Yeah. Me, my hormones and I." She closed her eyes and shook her head. When she met his gaze again, the hurt was back. "I'm not your responsibility, Nathan. I can take care of myself and this baby."

Apparently, *responsibility* was one of those words that triggered a hormonal response. He tucked the information away and searched for something to say that wouldn't tap into that well of defensiveness she had going on. He was attempting to say and do the right thing without research and training to fall back on. It was like trying to move a canoe with one paddle.

He blew out a long breath. "Look, Cindy, I want you to have the best prenatal care."

"Why?"

The word *responsibility* came to mind yet again but it hadn't gone well either time. There was no reason to believe that had changed. So he rephrased. "Just so we're clear, I am going to be involved. Because this is my child, too."

She stared at him a long time before saying, "I guess this is a bad time to realize the flaw of sleeping with you to get you out of my life."

And then she really did leave. He sat there for a few minutes as the situation sank in. A baby. It hit him like a meteor dropping out of the sky.

His baby.

Right now his child was growing inside her.

Holy crap.

An hour ago Nathan had been talking to Cindy and now he stood in the NICU at Mercy Medical Center, staring at a baby small enough to fit in the palm of his hand.

An infinitesimal embryo formed from his DNA and Cindy's was actually growing into a baby. He just couldn't wrap his head around the concept and make it real. Especially with the beeps, whooshes and noises of the high-tech sensitive equipment filling the room. This was where babies ended up when there was a problem pregnancy.

"Why are you still here?"

Nathan turned at the sound of the familiar female voice. "Hi, Annie."

The petite, blue-eyed brunette was his medical partner in the neonatology practice. They'd met in school and become friends. She'd introduced him to his late wife and was one of the select few who didn't blame him when the relationship unraveled just before Felicia died. He knew the failures were all his and would carry the burden of that for as long as he lived. This woman's friendship meant a lot to him, especially because he didn't deserve it.

Annie looked up. The pixie haircut suited her small face. "You know I'm on call this week."

"Yeah. I just wanted to come back and check up on this little guy."

She glanced at the gladiator. "I just looked over his latest oxygen saturation levels. The CO_2 and PO_2 results are all in normal range. He's doing pretty well for as small as he is."

"Yeah. I read his chart."

"Respiratory therapy was just here to check the ventilator. It's all good, Nathan."

"I'm worried about a bowel perforation."

"You're always concerned about that. I am, too." She settled her hands on her hips and slanted a puzzled look at him. "But something's up."

"What makes you say that?" Was it tattooed on his forehead? One-night stand? Father-to-be?

"This is me," she said. "Don't even try to pretend I don't know you better than you know yourself."

He was pretty sure she was right about that and felt a little sorry for her. Because she was wasting her time on him. "Nothing's going on."

"Oh, please." She huffed out a breath. "I'll buy you a cup of coffee and we can talk."

"Buy?" He stared at her. "Really?"

"Okay. Technically, I'll pour. Doctor's dining room. Now."

Nathan looked at the infant, the tiny chest moving up and down with help from the ventilator. "I don't know. What if he needs—"

"Don't go there. The 'what-ifs' will make you crazy."

He shook his head. "Maybe we should—"

"Look, Nathan, we'll be right downstairs. If anything happens we can be here in a minute or less. On the really bright side—" She smiled tenderly at the baby who couldn't see her. "This little boy gets two neonatal specialists for the price of one because you're going schizoid on me. You need to talk. I know that look."

"Okay." From knowing her a long time he knew that it was easier to give in than argue and lose.

They headed to the dining room on the first floor of the hospital. It was reserved for the doctor's use and available twenty-four hours a day. The tables were covered with white cloths and there was always one urn with coffee and another containing water for tea. Sodas were packed in ice beside the table with hot drinks. At specific times the steam table held varieties of warm food, but off hours there were only pastries, muffins and fruit.

Annie went to get two cups of coffee while he filled a small plate with sweets. They sat at a table by the floor to ceiling windows that looked out on Mercy Medical Center Parkway and the spectacular lights of the Las Vegas Strip in the distance.

Nathan bit into a brownie and realized he was starving. Lunch had been hours ago, and after Cindy's baby bombshell, food had been the last thing on his mind.

He finished the brownie and scarfed down a muffin, then noticed the expectant expression on his friend's face. "What?"

"Tell me what's going on."

"First you tell me why you're so sure something is."

She tilted her head and gave him an "oh, please" look, then sighed with resignation. "For one thing, you look just like you did when things between you and Felicia were going downhill."

Ironic. Before the baby, there hadn't been anything between him and Cindy except lust, but it felt like more than he'd ever had in his marriage. Felicia was a wonderful woman—pretty, funny, sweet and smart. They'd been friends and got along great. With his career on track, he'd figured it was time to get married. There was no lightning strike, but everything had pointed to them being a good match.

Only when it was too late did he realize that the logic was badly flawed and Felicia had left because he didn't love her. That was the last thing she ever said to him.

"It was a car accident, Nathan." Sympathy swirled in Annie's light-blue eyes. "Some idiot had been drinking and was going too fast. He didn't stop for the red light. That's why she died. It had nothing to do with the fact that the two of you didn't work as a couple."

"I know."

"That's not what the look on your face says." Annie sighed. "But I didn't bring you here to rehash the past. I want to know why you're hovering over that baby in the unit."

"I always hover."

"Not like this. Usually you're cool and clinical. That's not what I just saw." She must have noticed his protest forming because she held up a hand and said, "Don't even waste your breath."

"Okay. Don't say I didn't warn you."

"You didn't." She grinned.

He took a deep breath and said, "Cindy Elliott is pregnant with my child."

"What?" Annie blinked. "Who?"

"She works in housekeeping here at the hospital."

"I didn't know you were seeing anyone."

If just seeing her was all he'd done there wouldn't be a baby. Seeing her had only made him want her. Wanting her had made him determined to have her. He couldn't even say he'd been irresponsible. After seeing her earlier, he *could* say that having her once had definitely not made the wanting disappear. If anything, his hunger for her was stronger.

Nathan took a sip of coffee, then set the cup back on the saucer. "I met her at the hospital fundraiser."

"But you said she works here."

"Right." He dragged his fingers through his hair. "I didn't recognize her in a different environment."

"You mean all dressed up." Annie's look oozed pity. "Bet that didn't go over well."

"You'd win that bet." He laughed, remembering their verbal sparring that night and how clueless he'd been. It wouldn't add anything to this story if he shared that the smell of Cindy's perfume gave away her identity. "I asked for her phone number, but she refused to give it up."

"Ah." Annie held the coffee cup and her eyes sparkled with amusement that escaped him.

"What does that mean?"

"So many things, so little time." Turning serious, she said, "You obviously got together in spite of not being able to call her."

"Because I saw her here, there was no need for the number. I asked her out and we went to dinner."

There was also no need to share that Cindy had agreed to see him in order to get him to back off. Now he knew that was about the jerk who used her. He wondered if having that information would have cooled his jets, then he figured probably not.

"And you're sure the baby is yours?"

"The condom broke," he said.

Perplexed, Annie shook her head. "Isn't it amazing? We can build a space station and put people on it, but no one can manufacture glitch-free birth control."

"Go figure." He stared at the crumbs on his plate.

"So that's the reason you're hovering."

He nodded. "I never looked at what we do from the father side of the fence before."

"I see."

"That makes one of us. The thing is, I'm a doctor. I know all the things that can happen. I know what can go wrong." He pointed at her, then himself. "We see babies every day who don't go full term. The chances of survival go down when they're born too early—"

"Don't think that way," she warned. "There's no reason to assume a healthy woman in her—"

"Twenties," he supplied.

"Right." She nodded. "With good prenatal care a normal pregnancy is the probability."

That didn't seem like enough to ensure a healthy child, he thought. "There must be something more I can do."

"You're going to hate me for saying this," she informed him.

"What?" he asked, bracing himself.

"Support Cindy emotionally."

If he had faith in feelings, Felicia probably would still be alive. Science was what he believed in. He wasn't aware of any scientific study that proved emotional support would guarantee a full-term, healthy child. "You know better than anyone that I don't do emotional."

"Right. If you can't see or touch something, it doesn't exist."

They'd argued this point for hours in medical school and finally agreed to disagree. "There must be something else I can do."

"Other than finding her the best obstetrician in the valley there's only one other thing I can think of."

He waited, but she didn't say more. "Are you going to share?"

"Make sure she has what she needs to minimize her

anxiety," Annie suggested. "Don't let her exert herself. The rest of it will just fall into place if you're supportive of her."

He wasn't so sure. Cindy had been pretty concerned about work, school and the expenses involved in caring for a newborn. "Are you sure that's enough?"

"Positive. Just physically be there."

Okay. He could do that. He was a doctor, after all. *Physical* was what he did. So, it was settled. While Cindy was pregnant with his child, he would be her shadow.

Chapter Six

Peanut butter and jelly had never tasted this good when she was a kid. Now she was going to have one of her own and Cindy figured that was the reason.

She took the last bite of the sandwich she'd brought to work, savoring the sweet grape jelly mixing with the crunchy, salty softness of the peanut butter. She was sitting in the hospital's serenity garden and savored that, too. It was peaceful, and she could use more peace in her life. Ever since she'd won that pesky raffle ticket, peace had been hard to come by.

She pressed the palm of her hand against her still-flat stomach and tried to really grasp the fact that a baby was in there. A baby fathered by Nathan Steele. Life as she'd known it would never be the same.

She was going to be a mom.

Part of her was starting to get excited at the prospect. The other part wondered how in the world she was going to do this on her own. Because, despite what Nathan had said to her about helping, she didn't really believe he'd stick around.

And she was pretty sure she didn't want him to.

At least he was honest, not trying to hide the fact that his birth control had failed. He'd only made a small blip on the blame-game meter when he'd hinted that she should be on the pill.

If only…

Because she'd sworn never to be stupid about a man again, alternative precautions and the resulting bloat and water retention had seemed unnecessary. Now she was looking at about eight months of both. Not to mention figuring out how to do it all and pay the bills.

"Hi, there."

The voice came from behind her. It was deep and familiar and sucked the serenity right out of the garden.

Cindy half-turned just for visual confirmation that thoughts of him just moments ago hadn't conjured him up. The blue scrubs, thick dark hair and serious expression equaled Nathan Steele.

"Hi." She wadded up the plastic sandwich wrap and squeezed it into her palm.

He sat on the wooden bench beside her and glanced around at the shallow pond with the bridge curving over it. Several benches and chairs were scattered around the area. Three sides of the hospital threw the bushes, flowers and grass into shade.

"What are you doing here?"

"I don't think I've ever been here before." His response didn't actually answer the question.

"So your showing up while I'm having lunch is purely coincidence?" If so, she was going to have to burn a candle or something to reverse her continuing bad karma.

"Harlow told me this is where I might find you."

Had he been looking for her? She didn't like the stagger of her heart when she made that wild leap. She couldn't go soft now. It was bad enough that through a horrible twist of fate this man had fathered her baby. One day he'd unjustly yelled at her and the next thing she knew she was pregnant. In between he'd refused to take a negative response regarding her phone number and she hadn't stopped him when he'd kissed her. But kissing him had felt too good and now there were consequences.

Again, it was probably better to confirm. "Why did Harlow tell you where I was?"

"Because I asked," he said simply.

Damn, there was that little heart skip again. She'd like to blame it on the changes of her body from the pregnancy, but that was probably not the case. How could this happen when she wasn't even sure she liked him?

That thought didn't even come close to stopping the pulse in her neck from throbbing, and her voice was just a little breathless. Darn him anyway. "Why did you ask?"

"How are you feeling?" Again he gave her a nonanswer.

"Tired," she admitted.

"Still nauseous?"

"A little."

He glanced at the brown bag on the bench between them. "Lunch?"

"Peanut butter and jelly."

He frowned. "Technically you're not really eating for two, but the embryo will take what it needs from you. Nutrition is really important to its development."

How clinical of him. A change from the flash of feeling displayed when he'd said this was his baby, too. That had melted her heart a little. Her bad.

"I did some research online. I know that eating right is the best thing for the baby." She met his gaze. "Protein is important and peanut butter has lots of it."

"Along with fat," he pointed out.

"It's a good fat. Better yet, it doesn't make me want to throw up. And it's not expensive."

"Ah." He nodded. "I just wanted to make sure this wasn't a soup and crackers week."

"You mean just before payday." She refused to be ashamed of her strict budget. It was digging her out of a deep hole. "As it happens, this *is* the lean week."

"Right." He met her gaze. "If you run short, I can help you out. Healthy food is usually more expensive, but right now it isn't an area of your budget that you should be downsizing."

"You're right." She said that because he *was* right, but it didn't constitute agreement to take anything from him.

"Have you made an appointment yet with an obstetrician?"

"Not just an appointment. I've actually seen the doctor, even though it still feels surreal to me," she said. She'd called the day after telling him, and Dr. Hamilton's staff managed to fit her in right away.

"Good. Prenatal care is the first line of defense to prevent premature birth," he calmly pointed out.

"I'm on it," she promised.

"Glad to hear that." He looked around the garden again. "It's nice out here."

"Yeah. Quiet. This is a nice break from work. I've been really busy today."

He frowned. "You have to be careful. Don't overdo. Take it easy."

"I'm pregnant, not an invalid."

The retort was automatic, but for just a moment this

conversation had felt like a fantasy. They could be a couple. He could be a guy sincerely anxious for the woman he cared about who was carrying his child.

Then reality reared its ugly head. She was carrying his child, but they weren't now, nor would they ever be, a couple. The truth was that he didn't care about her any more than she cared about him.

His concern was for this child. His job was saving the lives of babies born too early and that's all this was about. Clinical concern. Still, she could respect that and him. In fact, she respected him very much.

"I'm fine." She smiled up at him. "It's just nice to be outside in the fresh air. In the shade with the breeze blowing it's still cool enough to come out here."

"Pretty soon it won't be."

"I know." She took the tangerine from her bag and started to peel it. "It's probably a good thing that I won't get too big while it's hot."

He nodded. "The first trimester will be over before fall. That will be easier on you."

"Yeah." That sounded like a concern more personally focused on her. He got points.

"You need to get in a lot of fluids. Water primarily. To flush the amniotic fluid."

Again clinical. And cute. As they stretched out the topic of weather in Las Vegas she ate the segments of her fruit, grateful to have something to keep her hands busy. She was much more comfortable with him when he was in doctor mode or chastising her for something not her fault. When Nathan was nice and charming, it made her nervous.

She glanced at the watch on her wrist. "I have to get back to work."

"Me, too."

They walked back into the hospital and the coolness felt good.

"Where are you headed?" he asked.

"I have to get my cart, then the NICU is next on my assignment sheet."

He fell into step beside her as she moved down the first-floor hall on the way to Central Supply. All equipment had to be put away during employee breaks. Besides the liability of leaving cleaning products out in the open, there was the problem of obstruction in the halls and impairing movement of equipment and patients on gurneys.

Environmental Services was located next to Central Supply on the first floor. Cindy opened the door, then turned to Nathan. "Thanks for checking up on me."

"You're welcome." He pushed the door wider. "Which cart is yours?"

She pointed it out, then was surprised when he grabbed it for her. "What are you doing?"

"I'll take it upstairs for you."

"You don't have to do that," she protested.

"You're going my way. I'll drive."

There it goes again, she thought when her heart skipped. Three times since he'd shown up in the garden. Could it be she was actually starting to like him?

The glow lasted until they entered the elevator. Two of the nurses from the NICU got in behind them and noticed Nathan helping her. Hostility, like an invisible force field, backed her up against the wall beside Nathan.

"Are you on your way to the unit, doctor?" Barbara Kelly asked. She was a slim blonde, very pretty.

"Yes," he said, and the nurse pushed the appropriate button on the elevator's control panel.

Cindy felt as if she'd been caught cheating with another woman's husband, and it brought her down to earth with a thud. Lowly housekeepers didn't mix with medical royalty.

Nathan tested the weight of the cleaning cart and said, "This thing is heavier than it looks."

Cindy decided not answering would be best because she didn't want to give the nursing staff any personal information. Gossip spread through the hospital faster than the flu and the facts of whatever story was spreading were usually wrong.

"You need to be careful while you're pushing it," the clueless doctor continued.

Apparently he didn't get her *"silence is golden"* vibe. Fortunately, before he could say more, the elevator stopped at their floor.

The two nurses got off first. One whispered something to the other. Cindy couldn't hear what was said, but she could definitely translate the bitchy looks both of the women lobbed in her direction. The message in the toxic glances said more clearly than words that she had a lot of nerve violating the unwritten hospital social code and consequences would follow quickly and without mercy.

Wrestling the cart off the elevator, Nathan missed the communication.

Before he could go any farther with her cleaning stuff, she put her hand on his arm. "I'll take it from here."

"We're almost there. That's okay."

"It's really not. Please, just let me do my job or I'm afraid I won't have one."

"What are you talking about?" He stared down at her, obviously confused.

Cindy glanced down the hall where the two nurses had disappeared. "By now it's all over the hospital that you were slumming with one of the housekeepers."

"What? Just because I gave you a hand?"

"And showed concern," she agreed.

"For that they're going to take me out back and shoot me?"

"Not you. Me," she clarified.

"You're joking."

"If only."

It wasn't pretty, but that didn't make the reality any less true. Bullies grew up but they didn't always lose their pick-on-the-peons mentality.

"The thing is," she said, "you can do anything and no one will say squat. But I have the audacity of letting you push my cleaning cart and the you-know-what is going to hit the fan."

"I'll make sure that doesn't happen," he said grimly.

The fact that he didn't even attempt to convince her she was wrong proved that he understood the hospital's insular social environment, at least on some level.

"If you really want to fix this, just back off."

"That doesn't work for me." He shook his head. "Like I said, I'm going to be there for you."

She put her hands on the cart and met his gaze. "I appreciate that you would want to, but please don't. I'm serious. It could cost me my job."

She walked away and felt his gaze on her back. Right this minute his attitude might be completely sincere. And that was extraordinarily sweet, but it wouldn't last. She didn't have the best judgment where men were concerned, which meant that he must have a flaw that would surface when she was most vulnerable. With a baby on the way she couldn't afford to jeopardize her employment and medical insurance benefits.

She needed her own space, no matter how much she was tempted to take a chance that he was different from the last jerk.

* * *

Twenty-four hours later Cindy was sitting in her supervisor's outer office. She'd been summoned and there was little doubt in her mind that it was somehow connected to her being sighted hanging out with Nathan—Dr. Steele—yesterday. There were so many rules, regulations and laws in this work environment, not to mention an anonymous hotline for grievances, that complications and intimidation were fairly easy to pull off.

If it got to be too much, quitting was an option for some. But not for Cindy. The nausea grinding through her wasn't just on account of the nerves about facing her boss.

The door opened and there stood Dina Garrett. She was somewhere in her late thirties or early forties with sun-streaked brown hair framing her pretty face in a stylish bob. A tailored navy-blue suit showed off her slender, petite frame.

"Hi, Cindy. Sorry to keep you waiting. Come on in."

Cindy stood and followed her, then stopped in front of the desk. "What's up?"

"Have a seat." Her boss indicated the two empty chairs.

"Thanks." Cindy tried to look relaxed and composed, but that wasn't easy when it felt like there was a scarlet letter embroidered on her chest.

"So how's everything?" Dina folded her hands, then rested them on the desk.

Cindy considered this woman a friend. They'd socialized occasionally, and she'd had dinner with Dina, her husband Ted and their two daughters. She'd even attended a piano recital for one of the girls. A family picture was prominently displayed on the desk, and she felt a stab of envy at the smiling faces, the close-knit family.

That was what she wanted someday, but the dream

seemed doomed from where she was sitting. It was on the tip of her tongue to reveal everything, but she decided to proceed cautiously. Once this was out of the bag, there wouldn't be a way to stuff it back in.

"Oh, everything is fine," Cindy said shrugging. "You know. How are Ted and the girls?"

Dina glanced at the picture and smiled. "Doing great. Summer camp. Swimming. Friends over. When school is out it's always harder for a working mom to juggle everything."

Cindy was already afraid of what her future held and didn't really need to hear that. "Tell them I said hello."

"I will." Dina smiled and when it faded she went into supervisor mode. "So, I wanted to see you because I received a complaint about your work."

"Anyone I know?"

"It was anonymous," she explained. "But I'm required to investigate and wanted to hear your side of things before proceeding."

That wasn't a surprise. Her boss bent over backward to be fair and that required more time, energy and work hours than simply jumping to conclusions.

"I don't know what to tell you." Cindy gripped her hands together in her lap. "I'm doing my work the same as I always have." When there are no complaints, she wanted to add. Nathan was the only variable. "Was the accusation specific?"

"No." Dina leaned back in her chair. "Because this is you and your record is spotless, I'm inclined to believe there's no substance to the accusation."

Cindy's grip on her hands loosened and blood flow returned to her fingers. "That's good."

"But there's another reason I think it's without merit."

Dina met her gaze. "I've heard rumors. Specifically, gossip regarding you and Dr. Steele having a relationship."

"There's nothing—"

Her boss held up a hand to stop the protest. "I don't need details. Your personal life is just that. Personal. But it's my job to see that work isn't affected."

"It's not," Cindy assured her. "Nathan and I—what I mean to say is, Dr. Steele—there is no relationship between us."

"Okay. Your work has been exemplary from the first day you started here at Mercy Medical Center." Dina studied her and, going by past experiences, she didn't miss much. "I'm your supervisor, but you need to remember that I'm also your friend. It's a fine line to walk and I work very hard at not showing favoritism. But if you need someone to talk to, I'm there for you."

The sympathetic expression and the invitation for a confidence seemed to unleash the dammed-up feelings Cindy had been struggling to hold back.

"I'm pregnant," she blurted out.

"I see." Shock mixed with curiosity in the other woman's expression. Curiosity won. "Do I know the father?"

"Do you know Nathan Steele?"

"Really?" This time shock squeezed everything else out of her face. "He's the father?"

"I don't know quite how it happened," she hurried to explain.

Dina's expression was wry. "Then you and I need to have a conversation about the birds and bees. It'll be good practice for *'The Talk'* with my girls."

"I *know* how *it* happened." Cindy felt the heat in her cheeks. "What I meant was that I've seen him in the NICU, but he never saw me. Not until the night of the hospital fundraiser."

"I heard you won the raffle."

"*Won* is a relative term. I couldn't resist messing with him when he said I looked familiar, but he didn't have any idea who I was."

"Apparently you clean up pretty good, or at work you look like something the cat yakked up."

"There's a visual." Cindy squirmed in the chair. "He recognized me the next day at work. By my perfume."

Dina looked more surprised about that than the pregnancy. "Obviously that line worked for him."

"Not really." It was only a small lie. "He asked more than once for my phone number, but I turned him down."

"Something changed your mind because you're not the sex-in-the-supply-closet type."

Cindy was grateful for that unwavering faith in her. "I happened to see him in action saving a baby."

"Ah. The hero factor worked in his favor. It's very powerful female fantasy material."

"I still said 'no,' but he wouldn't give up. So finally I gave in to a dinner invitation." She decided to leave out the portion of the conversation where she offered sex to get him out of her life. That had not worked out as planned.

At least not yet.

"If I had to guess, I'd say dinner went well?"

Cindy nodded. "He's more charming when he's away from the hospital."

"No kidding," Dina said.

"It wasn't like that." Cindy didn't want her boss to get the wrong idea about him. "He just kissed me good night."

She also decided to leave out the part about him saying he wanted her sexy, sassy, smart mouth. And the part where he wanted to taste the passion she put into being so tough. It had surprised her that he understood her so well. Maybe that's what had pushed her over the edge into mindless passion, but she didn't believe he'd planned to seduce her. Although she'd been very wrong about a man once before.

"Neither of us planned for this to happen," Cindy added. "Precautions were…problematic. It's just one of those things. But I want to clarify that there is no relationship between the two of us."

"Okay." Dina didn't look away.

"I'm aware that the staff is gossiping. For what it's worth, I believe the complaint about my work has more to do with the social differences between us. Although on the surface the two aren't connected."

"Just someone lashing out," Dina agreed.

Cindy leaned forward in her eagerness to dispel any lingering doubts. "It's just talk. I told him to back off, so that should be the end of it."

"Don't be too sure." The other woman looked skeptical.

"If not, I can deal with this. I have to," she added. "I need this job. Looking for another one isn't an option because of the medical insurance. Pregnancy would be a pre-existing condition and excluded from another employee plan. I'm just barely scraping by now. I couldn't handle it if medical bills were added to everything else—"

Dina held up her hands. "Don't borrow trouble. Not yet anyway."

Cindy got the subtext. "Yeah. When the baby starts to show, I won't have to do anything but waddle down the hall to stir up trouble and start talk."

"Okay, let's hope this is the end of it. Probably whoever called the hotline is just an anonymous whiner," Dina said. "If there's anything else I can do for you, let me know."

"Thanks." Gratitude for her friend's understanding and

support brought a lump to her throat and Cindy swallowed hard before saying, "You've already done it."

Dina shook her head, an indication that boss-mode was gone for now. "Wow. A baby. How do you feel?"

"Not too bad."

"Have you seen the doctor?"

"Rebecca Hamilton," Cindy said.

"Excellent choice. That's who I would have recommended."

What a relief that someone besides Nathan knew and she could talk about what she was going through. For another few minutes Cindy shared the changes already starting in her body, the emotions so close to the surface, the fears for the future. Dina talked about her own experiences and the joys of being a mom.

When Cindy left the office, she was relieved about her job status but not much else. The last time she'd been involved with a man, he'd taken her confidence along with her money. Yet again her life had been complicated by a man and she had the nagging feeling that Nathan Steele could take more than her bank account.

But that wasn't going to happen.

Just talking to him could cause trouble and cost her what little she had left. To keep peace in the workplace, she needed to become as invisible as she'd been before that darn dinner where she'd caught Dr. Charming's attention.

Somehow she had to rewind and delete.

Chapter Seven

Cindy was in the kitchen looking in the nearly empty refrigerator for dinner inspiration when she heard someone at the door. It was rare for her doorbell to ring, especially in the evening like this. Uneasiness crept over her. After peeking out the window to see who was there, her uneasy feeling was validated.

"Nathan," she whispered.

For a nanosecond, she debated whether to answer, but her car was in the driveway. He knew she was there.

After a deep, bracing breath, she opened the door. "What part of 'back off' did you not get?"

Resting his hands on lean hips he answered, "And what part of 'that doesn't work for me' did *you* not get?" One dark eyebrow lifted as he looked down at her. "Do you always answer the door like that? Hello to you, too."

"Hi. Why are you here?"

"We need to talk."

Cindy folded her arms over her chest and wished her hair didn't look like rats had nested there and her cotton shorts weren't quite so short. And quite so cotton. They were practically see-through.

"I have nothing to say."

"Then you can just listen."

She wished he didn't look quite so yummy and tempting in his worn jeans and white cotton shirt. The long sleeves were rolled up to his elbows, revealing wide wrists and strong forearms. Since when had cotton become the sexiest fabric on the planet? In his case, if it was just a little more see-through she might catch a glimpse of his broad chest, and that would be really nice.

Pulling herself together with an effort, she said, "I don't want to listen. Go away. I'm looking for something to eat."

She started to shut the door, but his hand shot out and he flattened his palm against it.

"Let me take you out," he offered.

She glanced down at her no-one-should-see-this-in-public attire. "Do I look like I'm ready to go out?"

Something hot and primitive flashed through his eyes as his gaze lazily drifted over her. "Then we can stay here."

"I'm not prepared to feed company." Did her voice sound as breathless and needy to him as it did to her?

"That's code for you're broke, right?"

"It's the week before payday." Her whole life felt like the week before she got paid.

"So we'll order pizza. I'll buy," he added.

That was a really bad idea. The last time he'd been in her house they'd had sex and now she was pregnant. She wasn't sure if something worse could happen, but she wasn't willing to take the risk.

Before she could figure out a way to turn him down, he

said, "I can see the wheels in your head turning and before you use up any more mental energy, you should know that I'm not taking no for an answer. Just look at it as a meal you don't have to pick up the tab for. My treat."

He was a treat, all right. That's what worried her the most. But it didn't look like he was going away without getting what he wanted. She wasn't sure if his persistence was endearing or annoying, but at least she'd get a free meal out of it.

"Okay. I'll change my clothes and we'll go out."

"While you're at it, how about changing your attitude?" he called after her.

She heard the humor in his voice and couldn't help smiling. He wasn't giving her much of a choice, so she might as well make the best of it. The prospect of not sitting home all by herself and fretting about how she was going to make this baby thing work did lift her spirits.

Besides, what could happen in public?

Nathan sat across from Cindy in a diner near the hospital and watched her hide behind a large menu the waitress had delivered when taking their drink orders. If it wasn't the week before payday, there was a better than even chance Cindy would have told him to stuff a sock in his dinner invitation. He hadn't worked that hard for anything since his internship.

Determination had served him well then, but he'd need more than that to deal with this woman. She had a chip on her shoulder as big as Nevada and somehow he had to separate her from it. The challenge got his juices going.

Sooner or later she would figure out that he wasn't going away.

"Have you been here before?" he asked.

"No. Have you?"

"Yes." It was handy when he was working.

The restaurant had a black and white tiled floor, red Formica tables and matching upholstery on the chrome stools at the counter. Waitresses wore red and white pinstriped uniforms to go with the retro look. It wasn't Capriotti's, which was kind of the point. That romantic atmosphere had landed him in this complicated mess. Now that he thought about it, he'd worked pretty hard to get her to have dinner with him that night, too.

And now she was pregnant.

Wrapping his head around the reality wasn't easy, especially when she looked as slender as the night he'd held her in his arms. She'd changed into a pair of denim capris, but he really missed the shorts that left her legs bare. And the short, knit top that let him have flashes of the naked flesh beneath. Neither outfit gave a clue about her condition, yet he didn't doubt that she was telling the truth. Funny, but her prickly attitude and the order to back off landed squarely in the confirmation column. She wouldn't do that if she were trying to pull a fast one.

There was zero romance here in this diner, but he could still smell the intoxicating scent of her perfume, and that cranked up a yearning in his gut that had nothing to do with food.

He blew out a long breath. "So, what are you going to have?"

"I don't see peanut butter and jelly," she grumbled from behind the menu.

"How about a cobb salad?"

She peeked around the tall plastic and met his gaze. "Really? Salad? You promised me dinner, not gerbil food."

"PB&J is dinner?"

"In my world." She ducked back into hiding.

"Okay," he said patiently. "What looks good to you?"

"Banana cream pie. With a pickle," she added.

"If that's representative of your current dietary choices, no wonder you're nauseous."

Again, she peeked out from behind the menu and gave him a sassy look. "Just wanted to see if you were paying attention."

Ignoring her seemed to be a challenge he was unable to meet no matter how determined he might be. "I guess I passed the test."

"Yeah. But I was serious about the pie."

"That's a lot of empty calories," he warned.

"Don't get your stethoscope in a twist." She put the menu down on the table. "It just sounds good. That's not what I'm getting. The doctor told me about the pregnancy weight parameters. Twenty-five pounds or so."

The perky waitress—Jayne her name tag said—returned with their drinks. Coffee for him. Water for Cindy. "So what can I get for you two?"

"Club sandwich. Wheat bread. No cheese. Side salad with oil and vinegar." She handed over her menu.

"Hamburger and fries," Nathan ordered, doing the same.

"You're going to hell," Cindy muttered.

Jayne wrote on her pad and smiled brightly. "Coming right up. Let me know if there's anything else you need."

He needed to let Cindy know he had her back. Unlike his father, he was someone a woman could depend on. If the waitress could rustle up an order of trust, there'd be a really good tip in it for her.

When they were alone again, he looked across the table. "So, how do you like Rebecca Hamilton?"

"She seems like a good doctor." Cindy removed the paper from her straw. "I like her a lot. She's young, smart. Easy to talk to."

He agreed. They had worked together from time to time. Every once in a while Rebecca called him in to consult when one of her patients delivered a baby too early.

"She's thorough, too. So she probably told you that staying in shape is important for both you and the baby."

"She did," Cindy confirmed. "And isn't it fortunate that I have a job that affords me the opportunity to move around a lot?"

And she couldn't afford much else, he thought. Thanks to the jerk who used her and disappeared. Nathan was furious every time he thought about that. And he didn't like the idea of her pushing around the housekeeping cart.

"Aren't there exercise classes specifically for expectant mothers?" he asked.

"There are. And I'll do that in my copious free time, right between my job and administrative internship responsibilities."

"How about on the weekend?" he suggested.

"Right." She took a sip of her water. "I can do that because money grows on trees."

"I'll pay for it."

The words just came out of his mouth. What was it about this woman that made him want to fix things for her? It wasn't the pregnancy because the protective feeling had simmered inside him from the moment he'd seen her cross that crowded ballroom.

"No, thanks." She smiled, and for the first time since he'd asked her to dinner there was warmth in the expression.

"I'm only trying to help."

"Believe me, I noticed." She dragged her finger through the condensation on her glass. "And I appreciate the gesture. But I don't care for feeling pathetic, that my life is a bad B movie. And if this were a romantic comedy, you'd have proposed to me by now. But we both know *that* kind of offer would be out of character for you."

There was nothing wrong with his character. He paid his bills, didn't use women and never made promises he didn't intend to keep. "How do we know that?"

"It's common knowledge," she said with a knowing look.

Not to him. *"It?"*

"You're a serial dater, which by definition means anti-matrimony."

"So that's the current rumor at the hospital?"

She nodded. "Is it wrong?"

Damn right. Partly. He dated because he hadn't been very good at settling down.

"Yeah, it's wrong. Imagine that. A rumor making the rounds at Mercy Medical Center that's been twisted and sensationalized."

"Which part?" Cindy asked.

"I'm not anti-matrimony. In fact, I was married once." He saw her glance at his left ring finger, which was bare.

It always had been. After the formal ceremony when he and Felicia had taken their vows, he hadn't worn a wedding band. He'd given his wife a host of excuses about it getting in the way when he was working. Gloving up. Sterile procedure. But she'd seen through all the crap and realized the truth about him.

"You said *was.*" Cindy frowned. "Past tense. You're divorced?"

"No." He saw the look of surprise and clarified. "My wife died in a car accident."

Not long after she'd left him because he didn't love her.

She'd been right, but it wasn't about her. Love was something he couldn't make himself believe in.

"Oh, Nathan—" Cindy's eyes widened with distress. "I didn't know."

"Not many people do."

"That's awful. I'm so sorry."

"Don't be." The fault was his and so was the guilt.

"I can't help it. That's what happens when you hear rumors and believe them without question. I should know better than to listen to that stuff. There's so much talk and every time a story is told it gets—"

The words stopped as she focused on something behind him.

"What's wrong?"

"Two of the NICU nurses just walked in," she whispered.

"So?"

"Isn't it ironic that we were just talking about gossip?"

Her expression took on the same wariness the day he'd tried to help her out. She'd told him to back off or it could cost her job.

"I have no idea what you're talking about," he said.

"Rumors will spread like the plague. You. Me. Here. Alone." She put her elbow on the table, then settled a hand on her forehead, trying to shield her face. "Where's a really big menu when you need one?" she mumbled.

"It's no one's business but ours why we're here."

"In a perfect world that would be true. But, trust me on this, there will be talk."

Nathan looked up when the two hospital employees walked by. He recognized the nurses—Barbara Kelly and Lenore Fusano. The first was pretty, blonde and blue eyed. The other woman had dark eyes and hair. Also attractive. He nodded a greeting and they both smiled and said hello, then kept moving without acknowledging Cindy in any way.

"This is just great," she said. "And the timing couldn't be worse. I told my supervisor that everything was under control."

"What does this have to do with your boss?"

She met his gaze. "I met with her because there was a complaint about me. Anonymous. On the hospital's hotline."

Nathan glanced at the two nurses and saw them look quickly away. "What was the complaint?"

"Supposedly about my work."

He remembered what she'd said about her life getting more difficult when word got out that he was "slumming" with one of the housekeepers. Then she'd told him to leave her alone because it could cost her job. That remark was one of the reasons he'd felt compelled to talk to her. To reassure her that she had nothing to worry about.

"Someone complained because you talked to me?" he asked.

"No. Because *you* talked to *me*."

He hadn't really bought into what she'd said about all the social hierarchy stuff affecting her employment. But someone had gone on record and the paperwork trail had started. "You should have told me."

"Why? What can you do?" she protested. "I already asked you to leave me alone, and we can see how well that worked out."

He wasn't walking away and everyone should just get over it. Including Cindy. "Backing off isn't exactly my style."

"Then you're the exception."

"I take pride in staying friends with the women I've taken out," he said.

Cindy blinked at him. "Don't tell me. The serial dater rumors are true."

"I object to the 'serial' label." He rested his forearms on the table. "I go out. In fact, I went out with one of those nurses for a while. We're still friends."

Cindy glanced over her shoulder and tensed before meeting his gaze again. "Don't tell me. You dated the one glaring a hole through my back."

"I don't see anyone scowling in your direction. Barbara Kelly and I went out a few times. No big deal."

"For you," she said pointedly. "But this is going to be trouble for me. And it's not like I don't have enough on my plate already."

"You're being overly dramatic."

She shook her head. "Must be nice to live in fantasy land."

On the contrary. He was a realist. The reality was that the child she carried was his responsibility and he would take care of it. And her.

Whether she wanted him to or not.

The day after dinner with Nathan, Cindy dreaded her work assignment in the NICU. Facing the two nurses after being caught "red-handed" with a doctor wasn't something that would make for a relaxed atmosphere. There were no written rules, nothing in the employee handbook, but that didn't make it any less true. Anyone who crossed the line did so at her own peril.

There was only one thing she could do. Her job. And she did it to the best of her ability, ignoring the hostile looks from Barbara, who watched like a prison guard from her nurse's station fortress in the center of the large room. The unit was full of tiny babies, but all was normal and quiet. Nathan was nowhere in sight.

A small thread of disappointment told her she'd started to look forward to seeing him, which was a much-needed wake-up call. Her pregnancy was the only reason he acknowledged her at all. He'd all but confessed to being a serial dater. And to losing his wife, which could explain why he *was* a serial dater. Heartbreak could make a guy unwilling to commit.

But understanding didn't change the facts. By definition, seeing a lot of women meant that he had a short attention span and sooner or later he would disappear.

One thing about having lots to think about was how fast she got her work finished. She glanced around to make sure everything was taken care of and all her paraphernalia was picked up. That was when she caught Barbara's toxic look with the three Ds—disapproval, disdain and distaste.

"Ignore it," she muttered, turning away. "Be Switzerland."

The resentment would blow over when Nathan reverted to typical male behavior and showed more interest in a ventilator than her. Until then, she'd do her job and keep a low profile.

She walked out into the hall and replaced her supplies on the cart before unsnapping her "bunny suit." Just as she was stepping out of it, the NICU door opened and Barbara walked out.

Cindy's stomach knotted because her luck wasn't good enough for this to be a coincidence. She turned away and set the disposable suit on the handle of her cart, then picked up her clipboard and pretended to study her next assignment.

"I want to talk to you." The nurse's voice vibrated with antagonism.

Cindy took a deep breath and faced the woman, faking a calm she didn't feel. "Is there something you needed?"

"I need for you to concentrate on your job instead of your social life."

She'd always thought the nurse was beautiful. Not anymore. The woman's mouth pulled tight, making her chin, cheeks and nose sharper, more Wicked Witch of the West. The coldness rolling off her made Cindy wish for wool socks and a parka. But a confrontation required at least two, and she was determined not to take the bait. That meant bottling up a whole lot of outrage and indignation.

"I'm sorry. I thought I was thorough in the unit. Did I miss something?"

"Yeah." Barbara folded her arms over her chest. "You missed the part where you keep your nose out of other people's business."

Cindy knew that "business" meant Nathan Steele. She decided to play as dumb as this woman desperately wanted her to be. "I don't know what you mean."

"Oh, please. Since when does a neonatologist push a housekeeping cart?" she asked sarcastically. "And take you to dinner. Isn't he a little out of your league?"

The knots in Cindy's stomach tightened, then cramps started in her lower abdomen. She resisted giving in to it. Show no weakness.

"Dr. Steele and I are nothing more than friends." And parents-to-be, she thought. But that "business" she was keeping to herself for as long as possible.

"Right. And next you'll be trying to sell me beachfront property in Arizona."

Cindy shrugged. "Ask him if you don't believe me."

Anger flared hot in the other woman's eyes because they both knew she couldn't and wouldn't do that. Barbara jabbed her index finger in the air. "Look, just because you won a seat at the big table, don't go shining up your glass slippers for a walk down the aisle with Nathan Steele."

Cindy wanted so badly to ask if this was junior high and Barbara had dibs on him, but that would just prolong this awful scene and the pain in her stomach was getting worse.

"I've heard he goes through women at the speed of light. It's really nice of you to warn me."

Barbara's fingers curled into her palms and the frustration seemed to roll off her in waves before she turned without another word and went back into the unit. Chalk one up for the peon, Cindy thought.

But the brief feeling of triumph was cut short by a cramping pain that had her sucking in air before leaning against the wall. She took deep breaths and waited for it to pass. The discomfort eased but didn't disappear and she very much needed to sit down.

She made sure her cart was flush against the wall and not impeding the flow of traffic in the hall. Slowly she walked around the corner to the empty NICU waiting room and tentatively lowered herself into a chair, folding her arms protectively over her abdomen.

She'd never felt more alone or scared, not even after losing her father. Something wasn't right, but she didn't know what to do. Finally she took out her cell phone and called her supervisor. A few minutes later, Dina hurried around the corner.

"What's wrong?" she asked.

"This is Mercy Medical Center. I figured by the time you got here you'd already know," Cindy answered, trying to joke her way into being brave.

Dina sat down beside her. "Did something happen?"

"Before or after Barbara Kelly got on my case?"

The other woman angrily shook her head. "She's not happy unless she's complaining about something. Or someone."

"Then she must be ecstatic right now." Cindy winced.

Concern went up a notch in Dina's eyes. "Tell me what's going on. You're white as a sheet."

"I think—" Cindy's voice caught and she bit her lip. "I have cramps. I'm just sitting here until they go away. I thought you should know in case someone says something about it."

"How long?"

"Just until the pain stops."

"No." Dina shook her head impatiently. "When did the pains start?"

"About fifteen minutes ago."

"It could be nothing," Dina said. "And probably is. But that's a chance you don't want to take. You need to call your doctor."

"I will," she said, nodding. "But it's getting better. When my shift is over, I'll—"

"Don't worry about that." Dina waved a hand dismissively. "You need to find out right away whether or not there's something to be concerned about. We're talking about your child's welfare."

Her child.

Her baby.

Cindy rested her hand on her stomach. There was a life in there. A life that could be in jeopardy. Fear rolled through her and cleared away the doubts.

In that instant, what had been a surreal, intangible, complicated problem became crystal clear.

There was nothing more important than her child. There was nothing she wanted more than this baby.

Nothing.

She would do whatever was necessary and everything in her power to protect it.

Chapter Eight

Nathan rang Cindy's doorbell for the third time. He knew she was in there; her car was in the driveway. If she didn't answer in the next thirty seconds, he would break in.

Finally the door opened and she stood there in shorts and an oversize T-shirt. Her eyes were red-rimmed, as if she'd been crying.

"What's wrong?" he asked.

"This showing up unannounced is getting to be a bad habit," she said, not actually answering the question.

"So is not calling me."

"Why are you here?"

"Dina Garrett told me you left work early. And why." He'd broken speeding laws getting over here after hearing.

"You went to my supervisor?"

"Because I couldn't find you and no one had seen you. It wasn't time for your shift to be over and you're not the irresponsible type. I figured your immediate boss would know what was going on."

"Oh."

Yeah. The woman had looked at him as if he were an ax murderer. Dina was very protective. Apparently Cindy inspired that feeling in someone besides him.

"So… Did you see the doctor?"

Tears welled in her eyes as she nodded without embellishing.

"And?" he prompted.

"I was cramping. She was concerned. I'm on bed rest for a few weeks."

That meant the pregnancy was still viable and the baby was okay. Relief washed through him, followed by anger.

"Why didn't you call me?" he demanded. "I'm a doctor."

"Not mine," she countered.

"I have every right to know what's going on." He would have driven her to the office. Been there to support her. But she kept shutting him out and that pissed him off.

"If there had been anything to tell you, I would have. Now, if you don't mind, I'm supposed to stay off my feet. And not worry about anything—" Her voice caught and she put a hand over her mouth.

Nathan swore under his breath as he lifted her into his arms and shouldered the door closed.

"What are you doing?" she demanded.

"Getting you off your feet." He looked around the room. There was a small sofa, a wooden rocking chair and not much else. "I'm taking you to bed."

"Put me down." There was an edge to her voice.

"I didn't mean that." Not really. Not now that the pregnancy had turned risky. But before this, the thought had crossed his mind more than once. "That didn't come out right. I'm going to put you in bed."

"The love seat is fine."

He glanced at it, a green overstuffed little sofa with tiny yellow and coral flowers. The first time he'd been here, having Cindy had been his only focus. Then he found out the condom broke and other details about the room disappeared. Now he took it all in.

The floor was wood, a medium-tone pine. A stand in the corner of the room held a small old TV. By the front door was a tiny mahogany occasional table with a mirror above it, right next to where he'd backed her against the wall and taken her. A bed would have been nice, but he couldn't wait. And he couldn't regret the most mind-blowing sex ever. Now there was going to be a baby. His responsibility was to take care of the mother in his arms.

That was why he was here. Because of the child.

In front of the love seat there was a cedar chest with a coaster and a glass of water. Five wadded-up tissues were scattered over the scratched and scarred top of the wood. She *had* been crying.

He walked over to the love seat and gently set her down. Now he felt the need to do more. To fix something. "Are you hungry?"

"No."

"Did you eat lunch?"

"A little."

That didn't sound good. "I'll fix you something."

"I haven't been to the grocery store." Her eyes filled with tears again.

Nathan moved the glass out of the way, handed her a tissue, then sat on the cedar chest across from her. "Talk to me, Cindy."

She dabbed at her eyes with the tissue. "I'd just finished my assignment in the NICU and started cramping."

He knew from Dina that there'd been a confrontation with one of the NICU nurses just before Cindy doubled over. That made him want to put his fist through the wall. She had tried to tell him, but he'd blown her off.

"Go on."

"The pains wouldn't go away and I got scared and called the doctor. She did a thorough exam and said everything looks okay. That probably extreme tension caused the episode. Then she said to be on the safe side I should stay off my feet for a few weeks. Then we'll reevaluate after the pregnancy stabilizes."

He nodded. All good advice. Err on the side of caution. Every doctor takes an oath and vows to "first do no harm."

"Then rest is what you should do."

"In a perfect world," she cried.

"You're not seriously thinking about ignoring her advice."

"No, but—"

"What?" he demanded.

"The Family Medical Leave Act will preserve my job, but if I don't work, I don't get paid. Without money I can't pay my bills. I'm terrified for the baby, but what am I going to do?"

"First, you're going to calm down," he said, concerned that she was working herself up. "Then you're going to let me help you."

"I can't let you do that."

"I can afford it." Chump change for him.

"This isn't your problem. It's mine," she protested.

"You didn't get pregnant by yourself. I want to do something."

"I'll figure it out. But I appreciate the offer. Really." She reached over and touched his hand.

His skin burned where her fingers squeezed, and the contact threatened to fry his concentration. He shook his head and struggled to focus. She needed his help. Because not working would give her lots of time to stress over everything she couldn't pay. But if he'd learned anything since getting to know her it was that stubborn was her middle name. Picking a fight over how he could help wouldn't be following her doctor's orders. So he had a better idea.

"You'll move in with me," he said. "The pantry, fridge and freezer are full. You can eat pickles and ice cream to your heart's content. I'm in and out, but I can monitor your condition—"

"No."

Nathan waited for more and when she didn't elaborate, he tried to figure out what was going through her mind. "I have lots of room."

"It's not about that." She folded her hands in her lap.

"Then what's wrong with the plan?"

"So many things, so little time." Her answer was no answer at all.

Nathan stared at her—the big, beautiful eyes looked bruised and battered. Her full mouth with its defined upper lip trembled. The escalating need to pull her into his arms made him increasingly uncomfortable. But it wasn't just because he wanted to comfort her. The truth was that if she wasn't on doctor-ordered bed rest, he might have carried her to bed and made love to her properly.

Her spirit and courage in the face of adversity were admirable and he should be grateful that she was giving him an out. Every instinct he had urged him to take it and run like hell, but he wouldn't turn his back on his kid, like his parents had with him. He was determined to be there and make the environment safe for his child.

To do that, he had to first of all not argue with the woman carrying that child. She'd drawn a line in the sand, so he had to find a way around it.

"Okay. We'll stay here then."

Some of the bruising left her eyes when suspicion replaced it. "We?"

"You won't come to my house and I'm not leaving you alone. That means I'm not leaving."

"You can't do that."

"Why?"

"I didn't invite you," she said.

"With all due respect," he answered, "how are you planning to stop me?"

"Logistics for one thing." She folded her arms over her chest. "There's nowhere for you to sleep. Certainly not in my room."

"Never crossed my mind," he lied.

"And the other two bedrooms are set up for an office and storage."

He shrugged. "Don't worry about me. I'm a big boy. Been taking care of myself for a long time."

"Nathan, no—"

He shushed her with a finger to her lips, and the touch seemed to shock her into silence. "You're not supposed to worry. So, forgive my bluntness, but shut up and relax."

Three days later Cindy wasn't exactly relaxed, but that was less about pregnancy and more about Nathan invading her space. It was early in the morning and she was still in bed, putting off getting up because she knew he was still there. Nathan had spent every moment he wasn't at the hospital in her house. Every morning since he'd refused to go away she'd walked out of her bedroom and peeked into the living room expecting him to be gone. And every day he wasn't.

Yet she knew he couldn't keep this up. He was a guy. Sooner or later he'd get bored with her as his latest charity case and bail. She wished he would get it over with—before she got used to him. Before it would hurt like crazy when she found out she'd been right, before she was alone again and less prepared to be that way.

Maybe she was borrowing trouble. Maybe today was the day he'd be gone. Today would be okay because she was ready for it, expecting him to disappear.

She threw the sheet off and slid out of the queen-size bed. After stopping in the bathroom, she tiptoed down the hall and through the kitchen. Peeking around the corner, she first saw his feet, then the rest of him dressed only in boxers. There was a sheet on the couch and he was still asleep, but probably that was from complete exhaustion. The sofa wasn't anywhere big enough to accommodate him, yet there he still was.

He looked a little dangerous, she thought, and a lot dashing with the shadow of stubble on his jaw. He was all rumpled, sleepy, sex appeal, and an unmistakable tug on her heart made her hope this was the last time she would find him here.

His eyelids flickered and he stretched, then suddenly sat up when he saw her. "Are you okay?"

"Fine." In the physical sense that was true because there was no more cramping. But emotionally she was a mess.

"You're not supposed to be on your feet. Are you hungry?"

"Yes," she admitted, admiring the expanse of broad male chest covered with a dusting of dark hair.

"I'll make breakfast. Go back to bed," he ordered.

After three days she knew resistance was futile, so she went back to bed. Before long the smell of eggs, turkey sausage, potatoes and toast drifted to her. Over her protests he'd grocery shopped and stocked her pantry. She had to admit the delicious aromas made her mouth water.

Then Nathan appeared in her doorway. He'd dressed in jeans and a T-shirt, but his feet were still bare, his hair rumpled and the stubble unshaved. He held a food-filled tray, and she held in an appreciative sigh. Her mouth was watering, but it had nothing to do with the food.

"Breakfast is served." He set the tray on her legs and started to leave.

"Can I talk to you, Nathan?"

"Sure." The bed dipped from his weight when he sat on the edge, just inches from her leg. "What's up?"

"This isn't working."

He frowned. "I can make something else for breakfast—"

"No. I mean this arrangement. You have to be exhausted from not having a bed to sleep in."

"I have to admit I'm not lovin' the love seat."

"That's what I'm talking about." Sort of. She had to convince him to go away. "And I don't need you hovering over me. I haven't had any more cramping. So, really, you can go back to your place."

"I'd like that," he agreed. Much too easily. "On one condition."

"Anything."

"You come, too." He must have seen her start to protest because he held up a hand. "It has more room and everyone would have an actual bed to sleep in."

"Don't think I'm not appreciative because I am." Except for her family and three best friends, no one had ever been there for her like this. "But this is my home."

"Okay. No problem." He rubbed a hand across his chin. "Maybe I'll pick up an air mattress. My mother will understand why I'm not at the house."

"Your mother?"

"She dropped in unexpectedly. She does that sometimes," he said.

"You should go be with her. No need to babysit me."

A gleam slid into his eyes. "Actually, you'd be doing me a big favor if you moved in. Mom and I could use a buffer."

"You're not close?"

His mouth pulled tight. "She has her own interests."

Shouldn't her interests include being with her son? None of her business, Cindy thought. "I wouldn't want to intrude. It would be such an inconvenience."

"Look, Cindy, I'm serious about Mom and me needing someone to take the edge off. But here's the bottom line. You and I both want the baby to be healthy. That depends on your ability to stay off your feet and reduce your stress level. I intend to make that happen. Where it happens is up to you."

She knew when to say when. Stalemate. Impasse. Someone had to blink, and apparently it would be her. She couldn't stand the thought of him being completely exhausted because she was too stubborn to compromise. There were other babies and parents depending on him.

"All right," she said. "Your place it is."

Nathan pulled into the driveway of his really big house before Cindy had time to process that she'd actually agreed to move in with him. He'd packed her things and wouldn't let her lift a finger, which was seven different kinds of sweet.

Now here they were. Parked beside a BMW SUV in his

driveway. It was a reminder that he already had a guest. Her stomach clenched.

"Did you tell your mother about the baby? Does she know you're bringing me here?"

"Yes." He pulled the keys from the ignition, then looked at her. "And yes."

"Good." At least there wouldn't be that awkward moment where she had to stand quietly by while he explained the unexplainable.

When she started to get out of the car, he said, "Stay put. You're not supposed to be on your feet."

"Then how am I going to get inside?"

A shimmy of anticipation danced up her spine when she remembered him sweeping her into his arms to carry her inside at her house. But the romantic notion dissolved when he emerged from the front door pushing a wheelchair.

"Be still my heart." Cindy wondered what kind of damage was done when a romantic fool dropped back to earth. But she sat in the chair.

It was a beautiful June day and already getting hot, so the cool air that washed over her when he pushed her inside felt good. When her eyes adjusted from bright sun to the dim interior, she saw that travertine tile went on forever in the entryway. There were high ceilings with crown molding and pale wheat-colored walls.

An older but very attractive woman walked into the entryway. She was tall and slender with a short brunette bob. Her eyes were hazel, and it was obvious that Nathan got his coloring from his mother. And his fashion sense. Her white capris were crisp and spotless. The black and white striped silk blouse was trendy and fitted. Even her sandals coordinated with the summer ensemble.

"So here you are," she said, her eyes narrowing on Cindy.

Nathan's voice came from behind the wheelchair. "Shirley, this is Cindy Elliott. Cindy, Shirley Steele, my mother."

They shook hands and Cindy felt at a disadvantage in the chair. Even standing she would be shorter, but at least she wouldn't have been loomed over.

Nathan leaned down. "I'm going to get your things out of the car and put them in the guest room."

Moments later he walked inside with her two suitcases then disappeared down the hall. He returned and glanced at his watch. "I have to get to the hospital. Shirley, will you get Cindy settled?"

"Of course."

"I'll be back later." He looked down at her with a warning expression on his face. "Take it easy."

Nothing about this was easy to take, especially being left alone with his mother. But he walked out the door and it was just the two of them.

Cindy didn't know how to be anything but direct. She got up from the chair and met the other woman's gaze. "This pregnancy was an accident."

"So I've been told."

"I didn't even want to go out with him."

"Technically one doesn't have to actually go out for something like this to happen," Shirley commented, her tone guarded. "But why did you? Go out with him."

"He was relentless and I said yes to get him out of my life."

"Yet here you are in his home. So we can see how well that worked."

"I didn't want to move in." Cindy refused to look away, even though that's what she desperately wanted to do. "But he's so darn stubborn and he wouldn't leave me alone. He's exhausted and the only way he's going to get any rest is for me to stay here. That's the truth."

"All right then. Nathan is a grown man and knows what he's doing." Shirley glanced over her shoulder. "I take it you know your way around?"

"Actually, I've never been here before." Cindy stopped there, not wanting to explain the one-night stand at her house.

The older woman looked just the tiniest bit surprised when she asked, "Would you like a tour?"

"Are you going to make me use that stupid chair?" Cindy glared at the thing.

"I think that's about my son being overly cautious. Stay off your feet means don't do the trampoline or go bungee jumping, not be an invalid."

Cindy nodded. "I think so, too."

"All right then. Follow me." Shirley turned and started walking away. "This place has five bedrooms and a guest house. That's where I stay."

Interesting. Nathan didn't really need her to be a buffer between him and his mom. There was plenty of space for the two to peacefully coexist. This house was big enough for its own zip code.

Cindy noted that the living and dining rooms were separated by the wide entryway and filled with dark cherry wood furniture and fabrics in earth tones. White plantation shutters covered the windows. The family room was right off the kitchen and had a fireplace on one wall. A huge leather corner group sat in front of a gigantic flat-screen TV.

"My whole house would fit in this room," Cindy said, still in awe.

"The bedrooms are down this hall," Shirley said.

She pointed out the master bedroom at the back of the

house, and Cindy politely glanced through the doorway, although it felt like invading Nathan's privacy. The room was huge, with a king-size bed across from a sunken conversation area and fireplace. A little twinge that could be jealousy told her it was best not to think about all the women who'd no doubt "conversed" in here with him.

Across the hall there were two more bedrooms connected by a bath. Her suitcases were visible in the first room.

"This is where you'll stay." Shirley walked through the bathroom into the connecting bedroom. "This gets the morning sun. And there's that charming window seat. I think this would make a wonderful nursery."

Cindy glanced at the L-shaped desk with the computer on top. There was an eight-foot couch and a wing chair in another corner. Clearly it was set up as an office.

"It would certainly work. But I'm not staying here permanently," Cindy protested.

"But you and Nathan will share custody."

It wasn't a question except in Cindy's mind. If she had to judge by her experience, Nathan wouldn't be around long enough to share custody or anything else. But telling his mother that didn't seem appropriate.

"I believe children should know both of their parents," Cindy said diplomatically. "If at all possible."

"I'm glad you feel that way because I've jotted down some ideas for a mural in here." Shirley picked up a sketch pad from the desk. "Would you like to see?"

It felt a little weird, but, "Okay." She looked at the drawings of cuddly zoo animals on the first page. "These are too cute."

"Those are generic," Shirley explained. "The next page is cars, fire trucks, airplanes. Boy stuff. Then there's the sports-themed sketches. Followed by fairy tale characters and princess pictures. Nathan can make a decision when he finds out the sex of the baby."

"These are really good." Pretty amazing, really.

She flipped through the pages, each set of sketches more impressive than the last. Knowing whether the child was a boy or girl would narrow down themes, but they were all so adorable, making a decision wouldn't be easy.

"You're incredibly artistic," she said.

"Not really. I just had lots of time to practice." Shirley's pleased expression instantly disappeared.

Cindy felt guilty because it was the first time the other woman had smiled and something she'd said had made the warmth dissolve. "You have a lot of natural talent. I don't think practice alone would be enough to do this."

"It is if you have the time. My husband left me." She shrugged. "Because I wasn't being a wife, I had a lot of time to work on other, creative endeavors."

But you were a mother, Cindy wanted to say. If the marriage wasn't working, why didn't this woman's time and energy get channeled into the young son who must have been hurt and confused about his deteriorating family? She'd never understood before how priceless her carefree childhood had been but kept the revelation to herself. In fact, she didn't know what to say.

But not saying anything made this more awkward than watching Nathan explain their complicated association to his mother.

Shirley must have felt it, too. "I've kept you on your feet too long. You should rest."

Alone, Cindy walked back into the room where she'd be staying. The bed was queen-size, covered with a floral quilt and a striped bed skirt in green and white. A tufted bench sat at the foot with her suitcases resting on top. There was an oak dresser with a mirror over it and matching nightstands. Very comfortable and should have been cheerful.

Cindy remembered what Nathan had said about being an unaccompanied minor. She'd assumed both of his parents had demanding careers, but that wasn't the case. He was a handsome doctor, brilliant and wealthy. Yet she felt sorry for him. And that was stupid. It could potentially weaken the hard crust around her feelings. And that would be a disaster.

If she made it through this pregnancy and delivered a healthy baby, it would be in no small part because of Nathan's support at this traumatic time. She would be forever grateful to him, but they were having a baby, not a relationship. That's the only reason she was living in his house.

The emotional health of her heart depended on remembering that.

Chapter Nine

Cindy had always thought that leather belonged on animals, not furniture, but that was before she'd experienced Nathan's decor. All afternoon she'd been relaxing on his family room corner group. The cushy feel of the soft leather had changed her opinion. And the TV wasn't bad either. It had to be at least a seventy-five-inch screen. In her tiny house it would be too big, but this room accommodated it perfectly.

"So size *does* matter," she said to herself.

She was watching an old chick flick starring Steve McQueen and Natalie Wood. The TV was so big and clear she could see practically every pore in the actress's flawless face.

Glancing at her watch, she realized it was after seven. Shirley was out and Nathan hadn't returned from the hospital. She was getting hungry and wondered whether to go digging into his provisions. *Mi casa, su casa,* he had said.

Before she could decide, the front door opened and closed, then he walked in lugging plastic bags of groceries in both hands.

"Hi," she said. "Need some help?"

"This is everything." His eyes narrowed on her. "And you're here because of questions like that. Your job right now is to carry nothing heavier than the TV remote."

"Then you should be proud because today I totally rocked this remote control. It got an excellent workout."

He carried the bags into the kitchen and set them on the granite-covered island in the center. While he unloaded them, he asked, "How do you feel?"

She muted the TV sound before answering. "Good. Normal. No more pains. Not even a hint of a cramp."

"Excellent."

"I'm thinking it's okay to go back to work."

He was putting a box into the pantry and turned to stare at her. "Your doctor advised you to rest for several weeks."

"But I feel fine."

"That's great. And we want to keep it that way. So just relax and go with it." He closed the cupboard door. "Where's Shirley?"

"Astrology class. She was going to skip it and stay with me, but I talked her into going." He didn't respond and she added, "You don't seem surprised."

"I'm not. Shirley keeps busy."

"She showed me some sketches for a mural in the baby's room."

"Oh?" He put bananas in a cobalt blue pottery bowl on the island.

"They're really good ideas—for either a boy or girl. She's quite an artist."

"Shirley's had a lot of practice."

"That's exactly what she said," Cindy informed him.

She was looking for some kind of clue as to how he felt about that, but he gave her no reaction, as if he'd perfected not reacting. And really that information was need-to-know. She didn't need to. Nathan's relationship with his mother was none of her business. But the fact that he called her Shirley spoke volumes.

When the silence stretched between them, she asked, "So what's in the bags?"

He wadded up the empty ones and threw them in the trash. "Nothing now. But I got you peanut butter and jelly."

She wanted to go all mushy inside from the gesture but held back. "What kind?"

"Crunchy. I wasn't sure what kind you liked, but how can anyone not like crunchy?"

"Sound logic," she approved. "And jelly?"

"That was a tougher decision. I fell back on personality."

"How so?" She sat up straighter and tucked her legs to the side.

"Strawberry seemed way too cheerful, so I went with grape."

"You think I'm more sour grapes?"

He rested his hands on the counter separating the two rooms. "Am I wrong?"

"I think I'm a peach of a person," she said.

"If you don't like grape, I'll go back to the store and get peach."

"No. Grape's my favorite."

But how gallant of him to make another trip. Her heart gave an odd little skip that she hoped was about her "delicate condition." The warm, fluttery feeling in the pit of her stomach could be nothing more than normal for a pregnant woman. One could hope, anyway.

"What else did you get at the store?" she asked.

"Lots of healthy stuff. Fruit. Vegetables."

"I don't like broccoli." She rested an elbow on the arm of the sofa.

"Then you don't have to eat any. And in case you weren't kidding about the cravings, I got pickles and ice cream."

She'd never been much of an ice cream addict, but suddenly the idea of it made her mouth water. "What kind of ice cream? And please don't say Rocky Road to complement my difficult personality."

He grinned. "Cookies and cream."

"Sounds yummy."

"I'm sensing symptoms of hunger. What else tempts your appetite?" he asked.

"Peanut butter and banana."

"Coming right up," he said without hesitation or editorializing.

She watched him work, pulling out plates, bread, the jar of crunchy peanut butter and the bananas. A warmth trickled through her that had nothing to do with the baby growing inside her. If she had to describe the feeling, the first word that popped into her head was *pampered*.

And perturbed.

He looked so cute moving around the kitchen making sandwiches. A feast for the eyes as she watched the muscles in his biceps bunch and his broad shoulders square off on the task. She was uneasy because when she'd agreed to temporarily move in with him, her concern had been mostly for the baby but partly about him being exhausted. She'd never considered him hanging around with her and unleashing a siege on her senses.

"How was work?" she asked. Anything to get her mind off this personal turn her thoughts had taken.

"The gladiator is holding his own against the lions and tigers. But his prognosis is still guarded."

"Why?"

He walked over to her with a plate in each hand before handing her one and setting the other on the coffee table. "Because he's fragile and anything can happen. Do you want milk with dinner?"

"What are you having?"

"A beer since I'm officially off call." He rested his hands on lean hips. "But I don't think you'd better have one."

"It doesn't even sound good and probably wouldn't be the best choice for the baby." Talk about his work reminded her that he knew better than anyone the need for prenatal caution. That's why she was here. "Milk it is."

He nodded, then fetched and delivered the drinks before sitting down beside her. He was staring at the muted movie on TV as he took a bite of the sandwich identical to hers. To his credit, he didn't choke or spit it out. Also to his credit, he'd put apple slices and baby carrot sticks on each plate.

Cindy stared at her food. "Do you always eat like this?"

"Like what?" He took another bite.

"Peanut butter and banana. Healthy and nutritious."

"Never had this before. It's pretty good," he admitted.

Suddenly she was really curious about his usual habits. "What's a normal dinner for you?"

"I grab takeout on the way home from the hospital. If forced to cook, it's a steak on the barbecue."

"So you're doing this for me," she said, indicating the fresh fruit and veggies.

"Yeah." He crunched on a carrot. "It's the right thing to do."

To some men "the right thing" in this situation would be marriage, but he'd never brought it up. Maybe because his wife had died. Was that why he didn't believe in love? Because it hurt when you lost that special person?

At least he was honest, and that was refreshing after the jerk who'd done nothing but lie to her. And Nathan was a nice man. It was incredibly difficult to work up a heart-healthy amount of resistance to him when he was nice.

"What are you watching?" He took a sip from the long-neck bottle of beer.

"I was channel surfing." She wasn't sure why, but she felt the need to explain stumbling onto this old movie. "Came across this Steve McQueen, Natalie Wood picture. *Love with the Proper Stranger.*"

"What's it about?"

She took a big bite of her sandwich and savored the flavors mixing together. But the truth was that peanut butter did stick to the roof of your mouth and it took her a minute before she could answer the question. Long enough for the parallel between her life imitating movie art to become clear.

"It's a chick flick." That should put an end to his curiosity.

"Steve McQueen usually plays a tough guy. Guns and car chases. Why is he standing in the middle of a crowd holding bells and a banjo with a sign around his neck that says, 'Better wed than dead'?"

"You don't really want to know."

"If I didn't, I wouldn't have asked."

"Okay." She looked at the happy ending silently playing out on seventy-five inches of screen. "They had a one-night stand and she got pregnant."

"Really?" His expression said that he got the parallel.

"He's not the marrying kind but asks her anyway because

it's the right thing. And in the olden days it was quite the stigma for a woman to be unmarried and pregnant."

"I actually know that."

"She turns down the proposal. Stuff happens and when he gets to know her, he discovers that he can't live without her, but he's blown it big time. The bells, banjo and sign are very public, his grand gesture to prove he really wants to be with her. That he loves her. Very romantic."

"I guess." He set his empty plate on the coffee table. "If you believe in that sort of thing."

"Someone must because romance is a moneymaker at the movies."

"Oh?"

"Yeah. *Titanic* was the highest grossing movie ever. Until recently."

"The boat sinks. So what's your point?"

"Exactly that. Everyone knows the boat sinks. The only reason that movie was so successful is because there was a love story at the heart of it. No pun intended."

"Is it possible that the special effects pulled in the public?"

"Some," she admitted. "Did you see it?"

"Yeah."

"Why do you suppose Rose as an old woman threw that expensive necklace in the ocean?"

"Dementia brought on by advancing age."

She laughed. "That works. I just kept thinking if she didn't want it, she should give it to me. I could really use the money."

"But if romance is the heart of the movie, that scene is symbolic. One could deduce that love makes no sense."

"If you don't believe in love, far be it from me to try and convince you otherwise. It's not worth the argument."

"Good. Do you mind if I put on a ball game?"

"It's your TV."

And house. Love had no place in his life. She was grateful for the reminder because hanging out with him was fun but a bad idea. After what felt like an eternity of digging herself out of debt by herself, leaning on him would be too easy. It would also leave her vulnerable and with nowhere to hide.

However, since their one-night stand he hadn't made a single move on her. Maybe because she was pregnant, but more likely because he was so over her. That meant the attraction getting stronger for her was one-sided and made the obsession to fortify her heart just silly.

His lack of attention proved she'd been right about him losing interest when he got what he wanted.

Sometimes she hated being right.

Cindy sat in Nathan's family room with her feet up and looked at two of her three best friends, Harlow Marcelli and Mary Frances Bird. Whitney Davenport, a medical technician at the hospital, had to work because the lab was short-staffed. She was counting on her friends to fill her in on what the heck was going on.

The two who were present hadn't told her that, but Cindy knew. The four of them had met at the hospital's new-hire orientation. Though they all worked in completely different departments, the click of friendship had been instant. Since then, the other three women had pulled Cindy through heartbreak and the financial fiasco that followed. She'd been there for the others during crises of dating, declining parent health and anything else they needed. Now she had to explain to them the unexplainable—how she'd gotten pregnant and why she'd kept it to herself.

This morning Mary Frances had called Cindy's cell and demanded to know why she hadn't been at work. She and Harlow had gone to her house, which, of course, was empty. They were worried. Cindy had given her Nathan's address and invited them over for in-person details. This wasn't a quick, cell-call kind of conversation. Nathan was at work and Shirley had gone to a candle-making class at the astrology store.

The time had come to confess all.

Cindy sat in the corner of the big, L-shaped sofa with her friends on either side of her. "So, how have you guys been? What's new?"

"That's what I'd like to know." Mary Frances was a petite, auburn-haired Labor and Delivery nurse at the hospital. She and Cindy were the same size, and the fundraiser dress had been borrowed from her.

"Okay. Before we start, anyone want water, soda, juice or coffee? You guys hungry?"

"Yeah. For information. What is going on? Whose house is this? And when can I move in, too?" Mary Frances's blue eyes held equal parts of humor and confusion.

Harlow tucked a shoulder-length strand of shiny brown hair behind her ear. Green eyes that missed nothing were narrowed. "I think I can answer the who question. But the why is still a mystery."

Mary Frances slid forward. The seat of the couch was so deep, if she scooted back, her legs stuck straight out in front of her. She lifted her hands in a helpless gesture. "Someone please start filling in the blanks because I'm clueless here."

"This is Dr. Steele's house, isn't it?" Harlow tapped her lip. "Oh, wait, he asked you to call him Nathan."

"What? When did this happen? How come you know and I don't?" Mary Frances glared at both of them. In spite of her small size, she looked fierce enough to do great bodily harm.

"Harlow knows because she was in the NICU working on a baby and picked up on some vibes," Cindy explained.

"So, she's right? This is Nathan Steele's house? You didn't win ten million dollars playing Megabucks?"

"No, I didn't win money. Yes, it's his house."

"How come you didn't tell me about this?"

Harlow shrugged at the accusing look. "You've been busy. I've been busy. And I didn't know Cindy moved in with him. What's up with that, anyway? I guess you finally gave him your phone number. Or went out with him. Or both." She looked around the beautiful, spacious room that could be from a photo shoot in *Decorator's Digest*. "I'd say he got both."

"Please tell me her imagination is on crack and she's gone to the bad place for no good reason."

"I can't." Cindy glanced at both her friends. "I'm pregnant and he's the father."

Harlow didn't shock easily, but she was now. "That's a place my imagination didn't even consider."

"No way." Mary Frances shook her head. "It's a joke, right? You guys think I'm gullible, but I'm not falling for it. You know better than to do something like that."

"I'm not kidding," Cindy confirmed. "And you both are a little bit to blame."

"Someone needs to learn how to take responsibility for her own actions." Harlow tsk-tsked.

Mary Frances stared at her. "How do you figure this is our fault?"

"You guys did too good a job styling me for that dinner I won the raffle ticket for."

"What?"

"Steele didn't recognize her," Harlow explained. "She made him guess where he'd seen her before, but he drew a blank. Then she ran out of the ball and he only caught up with her because the heel on my shoe broke."

Mary Frances pointed at them. "Do either of you see the parallel here?"

"What are you talking about?" Harlow demanded.

"Fairy tales. Cinderella." She nodded emphatically. "Am I right?"

"He's a doctor, not Prince Charming," Cindy said. "And he doesn't believe in love, so that ball had nothing to do with him finding a wife."

"But we digress." Harlow looked at each of them to get their attention. "He bugged her for her phone number and I advised her to let him call but dodge everything else. Bob and weave until he got bored and turned his attention elsewhere. Clearly that didn't happen. Which begs the question. How did you get from giving him your phone number to... You know."

"Sex?" Cindy clarified.

"Yeah," they both answered.

"It started with dinner at an Italian place—"

"Not Capriotti's." Mary Frances slid a knowing look to their friend.

"Yes. How did you know?"

"Doesn't matter. Go on."

What did they know that she didn't? Cindy wondered. Although it wasn't really important because the final outcome was the same. "There was candlelight, flowers, wine and food."

"Isn't that always the way?" Harlow was their token skeptic.

"So you got swept away. I understand that. But what about birth control?" So spoke the Labor and Delivery nurse who every day saw the result of planned and unplanned pregnancies.

"The condom malfunctioned." Cindy shrugged.

"That explains getting pregnant," Harlow said. "But why are you here in his house?"

"I had cramps and some spotting. The obstetrician said stress can sometimes be a factor. She ordered me to stay off my feet for a few weeks."

"You have a bed at your house," Mary Frances reminded her.

"Nathan watched over me and refused to leave. He's too big to throw out and there was no bed for him. So I agreed to move in here temporarily. It's really sweet when you think about it."

"Don't go there," Harlow warned. "I know that look."

"She's right. It's the soft and gooey expression. The one that happens just before you throw caution to the wind," Mary Frances said knowingly.

"I'm not throwing caution anywhere." Cindy folded her arms over her chest.

"Oh, really?" Mary Frances lifted one auburn eyebrow. "You're not the first woman he's taken to Capriotti's."

"I never said I was. That was obvious when he was on a first-name basis with the waiter. Who also knew his favorite wine." Cindy blew out a breath. "Look, you guys. I appreciate your concern. Really. But it happened. It was an accident and he's taking responsibility. That's all this is about. He's helping out. For now."

She didn't need her friends to warn her not to count on anything but today. She warned herself enough for both of them.

"Why is it that you didn't come to us for help?" There was challenge and a little hurt in Mary Frances's blue eyes.

It was a very good question. Cindy wasn't sure she had an answer. She shrugged. "It happened fast. I knew there was a chance of pregnancy, but really what were the odds? Then I did the test and figured Nathan should be the first to know. And I was pretty freaked out. I guess I felt stupid about it all. Please say I'm forgiven."

"Of course." Harlow patted Cindy's knee. "What are friends for? Show me a woman and I'll show you someone who's made a big mistake with a man at one time or another."

"Doesn't mean you have to compound the situation by falling for him." Mary Frances patted her other knee. "Don't go gooey. Stay tough. Get an attorney."

"She's right," Harlow agreed. "It's a well-known fact that Nathan Steele is a good doctor but a bad boyfriend."

Cindy nodded. "I'm well aware of his flaws."

"Then our work here is done." Mary Frances looked at her tummy and smiled, a soft and tender expression on her elfin face. "So we're going to be aunts?"

"Yeah." Cindy put a hand on her abdomen. "Can you believe there's a little someone in here?"

"We'll throw you a baby shower," her friend said.

And talk turned to babies, night feedings, dirty diapers and how her life was going to change. As if she needed the reminder. Everything had turned upside down the night Nathan noticed her.

As they chatted, Cindy figured out why she'd kept this to herself for as long as possible. She knew her friends would give her a reality check, bring her down to earth. Part of her didn't want to feel the thud. The same part that wanted to stay in the land of denial. But she couldn't hang out there anymore. Past mistakes had taught her she could take care of herself, but it was comforting to know her friends cared. It had been stupid to hold back, and they'd forgiven her without question. They would be there for her.

Their loyalty included reminding her of the truth:

Nathan was an exceptional and brilliant doctor. He was also a bad boyfriend. It was up to Cindy to get over the if-only-that-could-be-different feeling.

Chapter Ten

"I don't cook and Nathan would not be happy if I let you do it." Shirley sat down on the family room sofa and set a big, fat Las Vegas directory on her lap. "I can, however, dial the phone. What kind of food are you craving?"

"Don't go to any trouble. I'm happy with a peanut butter and banana sandwich," Cindy protested.

In spite of the resolve her friends had instigated just yesterday, she realized a lot of that sandwich appeal had to do with Nathan making and eating it with her. She needed a refresher course in not setting herself up for a letdown.

"I had a thing for peanut butter and pickles during my pregnancy with Nathan." Shirley's smile was small and sad. "But as delicious as that all sounds, I think a meal is the way to go. What about Chinese?"

"I like it." Although not right now, she thought.

"That was distinctly lacking in enthusiasm." The other

woman studied her. "I don't have to read your astrological chart to know you're humoring me. Mexican?"

Just the mention of spicy made her stomach lurch. She put a hand on her abdomen. "Probably not."

"Italian?"

That brought back images of candlelight and atmosphere the night this baby was conceived. Whatever happened, it would always be a lovely memory.

Before she could respond, Shirley said, "We have a winner."

"How did you know?"

The older woman tilted her head and tapped her lip, never taking her eyes off Cindy. "You just got this look on your face. All soft and sort of glowy."

If she was that easy to read, The World Series of Poker was out of the question.

"What would you like?" Shirley was flipping through the phone book.

"I guess fettuccine alfredo."

"Coming right up. I'll make the call. There's a place not far away that delivers." Shirley stood and started to walk away, then stopped. "When Nathan called, he said he'd be home in a little while. I'll get something for him, too. What does he like?"

Apparently he hadn't shared that they'd had exactly two meals together before conceiving this baby. One was rubber chicken at the fundraiser. The other had been Capriotti's.

"He likes fettuccine alfredo, too. And caesar salad."

Shirley nodded. "Okay."

Pretending to read her book, Cindy heard the other woman on the phone in the kitchen, placing the order. Then there was the sound of glasses set on the counter and the refrigerator opening and closing. Shirley brought wine for herself and a glass of water for Cindy.

After handing it over, the older woman sat on the end of the sofa. "So, what do you do, Cindy?"

There was a whole lot more that Nathan hadn't shared. Cindy should have expected the question, but she hadn't. She wondered if he talked with his mom about anything. It was possible he only told her about the baby because the pregnancy had turned risky at the same time Shirley showed up.

"I work in the housekeeping department at the hospital," she said. "I'm also doing an administrative internship for my degree in hospital administration."

"Aren't you a little old to still be in school?"

Way to find the exposed nerve, Cindy thought. But she was only ashamed that being a fool had cost her time in getting an education, not that she was still pursuing the goal. "Personal problems delayed me. But I'm almost there."

"Ambition. Good for you." Shirley sipped her wine.

"It definitely keeps me busy."

"You'll be even busier after the baby is born." The other woman's comment held more question than statement.

How was she going to juggle her career and child care? Pay for it all? And a lot more things that Cindy could only guess at. Curiosity mixed with suspicion in Shirley's expression. That was understandable. On some level she must be concerned about her son.

"To tell you the truth, I haven't really thought that far ahead." She turned down the page of her book to mark the place then set it beside her. "I'll be able to finish up my degree before the baby is born. And I have medical insurance through my job at the hospital. I have a tight-knit group of friends for support."

"Your parents?"

"Both passed away," she said. It wasn't a fresh loss, but a wave of sadness washed through her that her folks would never see this grandchild. "I have a brother in school at UCLA."

"So, you're basically on your own."

"Yes. And I'll deal with decisions as necessary and make the best ones I can make."

"What about Nathan?"

"What about him?"

"How do you see his role in this?" his mother asked.

"Whatever he wants it to be." Cindy hadn't expected him to do as much as he already had. She also refused to picture the three of them as a happy little family.

"So, the two of you haven't discussed marriage?" Shirley swirled the wine in her glass.

They had but only in jest or sarcasm. In one of her least shining moments, Cindy had said if her life was a romantic comedy, Nathan would have proposed to her. But she knew what his mother was asking.

"No. We're not getting married."

Shirley's expression gave no clue about her reaction to that—either positive or negative. She nodded and said, "That's very progressive of you not to feel the need to marry because of the baby."

Cindy recalled the old movie they'd watched, filmed at a time when a baby out of wedlock ruined a woman's reputation. But men got a free pass, even then. The old double standard. If there was any silver lining in this situation, it was that no stigma would be attached to her or the baby. She would be raising this child as a single mother. But the question reminded her about his revelation that he'd been married before.

"From what he's said, Nathan shows no inclination to get married again."

Shirley's gaze jumped to hers. "He told you about Felicia?"

"Not much. Just that he'd been married." The information had been offered only to validate his claim of not being anti-matrimony. "And that she died in a car accident."

"Such a tragedy."

"Losing someone so young is just horrible."

"It was awful. They'd only been together a little over a year." Shirley set her glass on top of the table, then reached down and picked up an album on the shelf below. "Their wedding was just perfect. And so beautiful."

"May I see the pictures?" Cindy wasn't sure what made her ask. Maybe it was like the all-too-human reaction to gawk at a car accident or stare at a train wreck.

"Of course." The older woman stood, then settled the heavy book of photos on her lap.

Cindy opened the cover. There on the first page was Nathan looking ecstatically happy and incredibly handsome in his traditional black tuxedo. She'd personally experienced him in a tux, including the dance that had started her world rocking. Her heart had been beating so hard she could barely breathe.

What would it be like seeing him so tall and strong while he waited impatiently at the front of a church while you walked down the aisle in a white dress and veil?

Cindy turned the page and saw his bride. Her big dark eyes sparkled with excitement. Long black hair fell past her bare shoulders in the strapless, beaded wedding gown. The veil was attached to a three-banded, crystal-studded headpiece. She'd been a beautiful woman and was absolutely stunning in the photographs.

As she flipped through, there were countless images of the blissful couple at their reception. The white tent was situated on an estate with a bricked-in patio, a crystal-clear pool and an endless expanse of grass. Table settings of delicate china and crystal glasses were set up on white tablecloths. A photo showed the first dance as man and wife, cutting the cake, the happy bride and groom chatting with friends and family.

And just over a year later his wife was dead.

"Have you ever seen a more fabulous wedding?" Shirley asked.

"No."

"Or two people more in love?"

"They look very happy," Cindy answered, closing the book.

"When she died, Nathan blamed himself."

"Why?" She looked up and saw the sadness in Shirley's eyes. Obviously his mother had cared a lot about the woman her son married. Would anyone ever be able to fill that void?

"I've heard people say that it happens when you lose the love of your life. Although I wouldn't know about that since my husband walked out because he *didn't* love me." Shirley rubbed a finger beneath her nose. "Felicia was like the daughter I didn't have."

What about the son you *did* have?

Piecing together the little Nathan had said, she knew Shirley had buried herself in projects to get through a hard time in her life. Cindy couldn't help wondering how that affected Nathan. But it wasn't her place to judge.

The pain of losing someone you love could do funny things to a person. Some ran away from life. Others ran away from love. She knew which category Nathan fell into after seeing how happy he looked in his wedding pictures.

So the question had to be asked. Did Nathan not believe in love? Or was denying it existed at all his way of hiding from an unimaginable loss?

Either way, this little stroll down memory lane confirmed

that she was wise to guard her heart. It was unlikely that he was open to caring about someone no matter how much Cindy might wish he could care just a little bit about her.

Nathan had driven Cindy to Rebecca Hamilton's office and now sat nervously in the waiting room while the obstetrician examined her. Over the last few weeks, his initial fear for her and the baby had receded when there were no further symptoms. And without further symptoms it got harder and harder to keep her quiet and resting as the days passed. When he wasn't working, he was home with her, making sure she ate right and got enough sleep. The rest of the time they watched movies and played quiet board games.

Although quiet was a relative term. Cindy was a ferociously competitive Scrabble player and pretty darn good at gin rummy. She was anything but quiet when she beat him badly at whatever game they were playing. It had both amused and entertained him. Mostly he hoped that she was entertained and the enforced R&R had done the trick.

Sitting by the door that led to the back office, Nathan looked around the waiting area feeling like a fly in a glass of milk. He was the only guy, caught in some gray area of this crazy journey to fatherhood. Though he'd never experienced it himself, he figured husbands probably accompanied their wives into the exam room. Even men in a committed, intimate relationship would be allowed in with the woman carrying their baby.

He felt like a sperm donor, relegated to benchwarmer. It was damn disconcerting because he was normally elbow deep in the action and calling the shots. The urge to pace was pretty overwhelming, but he wouldn't give in to it. If Cindy didn't emerge from the back office bastion of femaleness, he would take the necessary steps to get any answers he deemed appropriate to his involvement in this adventure. Ten more minutes, he decided, looking at his watch to start the clock ticking on his plan.

Eight minutes and forty-five seconds later the door opened. Every woman in the waiting area looked up and so did he. Cindy walked out, and he studied her expression for elation or agitation. If she'd just bested him at Scrabble, she'd have pumped her arm and shouted "yes" as a victorious gleam sparkled in her brown eyes. When he beat her at anything, the gold flecks disappeared. Before he could decode the current color, she slid her sunglasses on and stopped at the reception desk a few steps from where he was sitting.

Nathan joined her there while she made another appointment, then settled his hand at the small of her back to escort her out. It jolted him how strong and instinctive the inclination was to slide his arm around her. But he stopped just in time.

When the office door closed after them he asked, "Well? What did she say?"

"Everything's fine with the baby. There's no reason to assume there will be any more problems. It just happens sometimes. All is currently well and I have her dispensation to resume all normal activities."

Nathan's mind went immediately to sex, not that it was a normal activity for the two of them. But the need was more than he wanted it to be.

She let out a long breath. "What a relief."

Yes. And no.

He was incredibly grateful that the baby was okay, but the risky pregnancy had effectively kept his mind off ideas he had no business having. Their situation already defied reason, and factoring in sex made it off the chart in terms of complicated.

The sun was hot when they left the medical building's courtyard, but visions of getting Cindy naked made his skin burn for reasons that had nothing to do with the UVA index. In the June heat, she wasn't wearing all that much— a little yellow cotton sundress and white sandals. He could put the flat of his palm on her belly and feel the way his baby was already changing the feminine curves of her body.

That was about the sexiest thought he'd ever had. The wanting that he'd been suppressing for weeks broke free and the only thing preventing him from pulling her into his arms and kissing the living daylights out of her was the way her lips pulled tight.

Something was wrong.

They walked through the parking lot and found the car. He opened the door, then handed her inside without exchanging a word. After he got in, he turned the key in the ignition to give it just enough juice to get the cool air going, but he made no move to drive anywhere.

"What aren't you telling me?" he demanded.

Cindy glanced sideways. "Nothing."

"Then what's bothering you?" He knew her moods pretty well now and something wasn't right.

"It's nothing really."

"Nothing really means it's really something. Tell me," he urged.

"It's just—" She caught the edge of her bottom lip between her teeth. "Resuming normal activity means going back to work."

"Right."

Right. Of course she would go back. He should have realized that, but when testosterone got the upper hand, rational thought didn't stand much of a chance. Tension from rumors and talk at the hospital could very well have caused her original symptoms in the first place.

"You know, Cindy, if you want to resign from your job, I'll support you through the pregnancy."

"What about after?" She was thoughtful for a few moments, then shook her head. "There's still my internship at the hospital. They gave me a short leave of absence, but the health of my future career is there, too. And, as generous as your offer is, I need a career to take care of myself and the baby."

"You don't have to worry about—"

"Yeah," she interrupted. "I do have to worry. I need to go back to my house and my job. I have to take care of myself."

"You're not alone."

"If you say so." Cool air from the dashboard vents blew the hair off her forehead.

It was probably his imagination, but he could swear there were shadows on the half of her face he could see. She looked small and scared. Nathan wanted badly to pull her against him, fold her in his arms and convince her it was okay to trust him. So the fact that this car was a small two-seater without room to act rashly was probably for the best. The only tools in his arsenal were words and logic.

"There's no need to be afraid of going back to work. I'm sure all the rumors have blown over by now."

"You don't really believe that, do you?"

"Yeah, I do. It's been a few weeks. Everyone's no doubt moved on to other, more interesting topics."

She shook her head ruefully. "No one questions your IQ creds, but street smarts are a different story."

"What does that mean?"

"You don't live in the real world. You're so many levels

removed from the rank and file that you have no idea how the pecking order operates."

"Okay. So explain it to me." He didn't walk in her shoes, but he wasn't completely oblivious.

"When I show up back to work, talk will start up all over again about why I was gone."

"Because you didn't feel well." He shrugged. "It's not a lie."

"Without details there will be theories from swine flu to shingles. Either or both will be taken as fact."

"So ignore them."

"I plan to. And hope it blows over and talk goes back to politics and how the new healthcare legislation will change things at the hospital."

"That's the spirit."

"Yeah, one can fantasize. But if the best-case scenario doesn't pan out—"

Before she could finish the negative thought, he said, "I've got your back."

"Absolutely, positively no." Her full lips compressed to a thin line as she shook her head.

Talking to her was old news. Coworkers did it all the time. "What's wrong with me being your friend?"

"You're a doctor and I work in housekeeping—"

"Environmental Services," he corrected.

"Whatever. If you acknowledge me in any way, or exhibit sympathetic behavior, anything that even hints of preferential treatment, I promise you it will get ugly. And I can't afford to get fired. On top of providing for this baby, I'm still digging myself out of debt from my last mistake."

Meaning that he was her current mistake.

Instead of responding to that, Nathan started the car and backed out of the parking space. Then he turned right onto Horizon Ridge Parkway. The second light was Eastern

Avenue and he turned left, heading for the 215 Beltway. Traffic congestion meant he had to concentrate on driving and couldn't lose his temper, which he really wanted to do.

But that wasn't fair to Cindy. She'd already been used and abused by a back-stabbing son of a bitch and Nathan fervently wished for five minutes alone with the jerk who'd swiped more than her credit. The bastard had stolen her trust and it made Nathan furious.

He was paying the price at a time when Cindy needed to believe in him the most. It fried him big time that she couldn't let herself count on him to protect her.

"Nathan?"

"What?" he snapped.

He'd turned onto the beltway and merged into traffic then pressed on the gas as the sporty luxury car smoothly took off and left the rest of the clunkers in his dust. This time of day there was very little traffic on this road and lots of open road in front of him.

"Nathan?"

"What?" he said again.

"You might want to slow it down a little." She glanced over at him. "You could probably talk your way out of a speeding ticket on account of being a doctor except for two things."

"Which are?"

"You're headed away from the hospital and I'm in the car. No cop would believe you've got an emergency with a patient."

He wasn't going that much over the legal limit, but he slowed down and set the cruise control. If only he could do that to the fury raging inside him. Losing focus wasn't his style. He didn't normally get this angry, let alone give in to the primal, passionate feelings.

Not until Cindy.

Nathan wanted her to let him help, to allow him to take some of the stress off her, but because of what that one moron had done, she was pushing back. Telling her he wouldn't let her down wasn't going to convince her that he meant the words, even though he'd never been more sincere about anything in his life.

He knew how it felt to be abandoned by the very people who should have cared the most. Now he was going to be a parent. He intended to step up even before the baby was born.

That meant he had no intention of abandoning Cindy.

Correction: He wouldn't abandon his child and she was the child's mother. Therefore he would be there for her.

It wasn't her fault that he couldn't stop wanting her. That was a perplexing footnote about this whole complicated situation because that had never happened to him before.

He always lost interest. To his way of thinking, that was significant data proving that love didn't exist. But Cindy continually surprised him, and sex was at the top of his interest list. Both did a number on his peace of mind, and neither were beneficial to him in the long term. When feelings started to get complicated in a relationship, he left. Because of the baby he couldn't do that now.

So, he had to keep things from getting complicated. He would have to prove he wasn't going away and at the same time keep Cindy from knowing how much he wanted her.

No pressure there.

Chapter Eleven

It was her first day back to work after Dr. Hamilton had green lighted her to return. Cindy was ecstatic about that *and* about returning to her home. Normal was good. Having her own Nathan-free zone was awesome. Earning a paycheck again gave her peace of mind.

At least that's what she told herself.

The morning at the hospital had been uneventful, if you didn't count her tense, awkward bathroom run-in with the two NICU nurses who'd made it their mission in life to keep her from getting uppity. Cindy had been the model of serenity. She'd smiled politely, taken a deep breath, then imagined herself enveloped in a force field that repelled everything, including the hostile glares.

Now it was lunch time and the first half of her first day was over. Without incident. Of course, she hadn't been to the NICU yet or seen Nathan. She could only hope that the seed of her warning to not acknowledge her in any way, and not give her a hint of preferential treatment, had fallen on fertile ground. He hadn't been happy, and she was sorry about that, but it couldn't be helped.

"May I join you?"

Cindy had been so wrapped up in her own thoughts, she hadn't noticed the woman stop beside her table in the back corner of the cafeteria. Dr. Annie Daniels patiently waited for her response with a tray of food in her hands. If she was here at the hospital, that would explain why Nathan wasn't. They were medical partners.

"Cindy?"

Hearing her name was like a shot of adrenaline to snap her out of it. "I'm sorry. Of course you can sit. If you want to."

"If I didn't want to, I wouldn't have asked."

Shocked into a response didn't mean Cindy wasn't still shocked. This doctor was a brainy, beautiful brunette with a stylish pixie haircut that made her blue eyes look enormous in her small face. The hospital had a special dining room for doctors so they weren't forced to mingle with the employees. Yet this doctor was voluntarily mingling. What was up with that?

Dr. Daniels had always been friendly, but she was that way to everyone. Never condescending or abrasive. But it didn't answer the question of the day: Why in the world would this elite female physician want to join her?

The doctor set her tray on the table and sat. "How are you feeling?"

"Fine." Feeling? That seemed kind of specific. Most people just said a generic how are you. And that's what she did now. "How are you?"

"Really good." She mixed dressing into her cobb salad. "But I'm not pregnant."

And that answered the question of whether she knew

about the baby. She was also Nathan's medical partner. Did she know he was the father?

There was nothing but kindness in her blue eyes. "And I didn't just return from a leave of absence taken because my pregnancy turned risky."

"Look, Dr. Daniels—"

"Call me Annie. If I'm going to butt into your business, the least you can do is call me by my first name." She smiled, then took a bite of salad.

Cindy chose to believe she meant that and said, "Annie, I don't mean to sound suspicious and ungrateful, but why are you butting into my business?"

"I feel responsible for some of the crap you're dealing with."

Color her shocked. Again. "Why?"

"The thing is, Mercy Medical Center is like a family." The doctor smiled at her skeptical look. "Don't get me wrong. I know it's a big, messy, dysfunctional one, but still a family. There are very few secrets."

"Meaning?" Cindy kept her hands busy peeling a tangerine and pulling off all the little strings.

"Nathan told me he's the father of your baby."

"I see." That was a big, fat lie. She didn't see anything. There was nothing hostile or toxic in the other woman's expression, but that didn't mean a zinger wasn't coming. "Why would he tell you that?"

"I don't think he planned to. But apparently he'd just found out." Annie speared a piece of egg with her fork. "It was my shift in the NICU, but he came back to check on a baby."

"Is that unusual?"

Annie shook her head. "But something was different and I sensed that. After a little nagging on my part, he admitted that he was going to be a father. And that he'd never looked at what we do from the dad side of the fence before."

"Okay."

"He told me about you. How you'd met. That he didn't recognize you all dressed up. And that didn't land him on your good side."

Cindy smiled at the memory. "I gave him a pretty hard time about it."

"Good for you. He needs someone to take him down a peg or two and keep him grounded in the real world."

"My world is all too real," Cindy said grimly.

"I feel responsible for what you're going through here at the hospital," she said again.

"What do you mean?" She stared across the small table.

"The tension and resentment other employees are exhibiting toward you."

Interesting that someone else had noticed, Cindy thought. That made it easier somehow. "But why do you feel responsible?"

"I overheard a couple nurses in the NICU talking and I decided to chat with you."

"I don't understand."

Annie poured sugar into her iced tea and stirred with her straw. "It all goes back to that night Nathan came back to hover over the baby. It's what he does. His job. Our job. We take care of babies who aren't big enough, strong enough or mature enough to survive without medical intervention."

Cindy pressed a hand to her abdomen. "It's a scary thing."

"Not just for you." Annie met her gaze. "A little knowledge is a dangerous thing because Nathan and I know all the things that can happen. The problem is he's a guy."

Not a newsflash, Cindy thought. He had the broad

shoulders and muscles in all the right places to prove that. If he weren't quite so mouthwateringly masculine, she wouldn't be in this fix in the first place. And worse, spending time with him at his house had not taken away any of his appeal. But she was pretty sure that's not what Annie meant.

"Why is that a problem?" she asked.

"Guys want to fix things. He's also a doctor. So when he was feeling the need to do something for his child, I had to talk him down."

"How?"

"I advised him to support you emotionally."

"He's not into that." Cindy popped a tangerine segment into her mouth and chewed for a moment. "When we met, he said that if he can't see and touch something, he doesn't believe it exists."

"So, you've heard his company line. He's a man of science. Facts and results. That's such a lame excuse and on some level he knows it." Annie sighed. "At any rate, I advised him to be there for you. Make sure you have everything you need to minimize any anxiety."

"It's good advice. I don't understand why you feel responsible for anyone else's behavior."

"I also told him not to let you exert yourself." Annie watched carefully and nodded when the truth sank in.

"He was taking your advice to heart. Trying to keep me from overdoing it here at work," Cindy said.

A man who actually listened. It also proved the saying "no good deed goes unpunished." Unfortunately, she was paying the price for his chivalry.

"That's right," Annie agreed. "The down side is that people noticed."

By *people* she meant a certain nurse who just happened

to be an ex-girlfriend. Scenarios didn't come more volatile than that.

"Noticing isn't the problem. But I could do without the ugly comments."

"I'm really sorry about that," Annie sympathized.

"Unless you wrote the script, you have nothing to apologize for," Cindy assured her. "There will be more talk when the pregnancy starts to show."

"Thanks to me and the ideas I gave Nathan, it won't be hard to put two and two together and figure out he's the father."

"Yeah." This wasn't the first time Cindy had thought about that. "It'll be fun to hear the creative ways they'll say how I'd do anything to trade up from housekeeping."

Annie pointed with the business end of her fork and forcefully said, "Ignore the small-minded…witches and their rumors. Whatever is between you and Nathan is no one's business but yours. And his."

"And yours?"

"I've known him since medical school." The lady doctor shrugged. "It's hard to ignore how well I know him."

"He's lucky to have a friend like you."

"I'm the lucky one." Her expression turned introspective and a little sad. "He was there for me when I lost my baby. It was a double whammy because to save my life, they had to do a hysterectomy."

"Oh, no—" Cindy reached out and squeezed the other woman's hand. The gesture was automatic, generated by a profound sympathy. One woman to another. She'd thought her problems were big and had to admit that all things considered the ability to have a baby was a blessing. "I don't know what to say."

"Thanks for not saying you're sorry. For some reason that response makes me want to scream. And I have no idea why I told you that." Annie shook her head. "Don't fret on my account. Thanks to science and other options my husband and I are exploring ways to be parents that do work for us."

"Your husband sounds like quite a guy," Cindy said.

"I won't argue that. Ryan is the best." Annie's eyes glowed. "And so is Nathan. Quite a guy, I mean. For what it's worth, the weird and wonderful chemistry that men and women feel for each other knows no boundaries—not caste, class or career. Take it from someone who knows—your energy is better spent taking care of you and your baby. To hell with the rest of the crap."

"No wonder Nathan talks to you." Cindy smiled. "Not only do you have a way with words, you give very good advice."

Annie laughed. "Nathan has been through a lot. Just remember that underneath all the geek and science stuff he preaches, he's a good man."

Annie suddenly pulled a pager from the waistband of her scrubs and glanced at the display. "Gotta go."

"Thanks for sitting with me."

"Let's do it again sometime soon." And then she hurried away.

Cindy had always liked Annie Daniels and the feeling was even stronger now. She was a good doctor and a warm human being who had little tolerance for small-minded people. From the moment Cindy had peed on the stick and discovered she was pregnant, her life had been in free fall. She'd never considered how it would feel to lose a baby and never be able to have another one.

Nathan had supported his friend through the nightmare. Actions like that and the friends in his corner spoke to the kind of man he was. The information troubled her because it would be so much easier if he had the decency to live up to his reputation of good doctor, bad boyfriend. Then her feelings could be black and white. She could dislike him. Dr. Daniels had just confirmed what Cindy had been suspecting for a while.

It was impossible to dislike Nathan Steele.

And what if she couldn't stop with just liking him?

Cindy walked barefoot to the kitchen after changing into shorts and a skinny-strapped tank top. She and the baby had survived the first day back at work. If you didn't count her conversation with Annie, it had been ordinary and nothing to write home about.

She wasn't sure what to do with the doctor's independent confirmation that Nathan was a nice guy. Theoretically the information shouldn't change anything. This baby was his and he was merely taking responsibility. The form that responsibility would take was yet to be determined. That being the case, she needed to move forward expecting nothing from anyone and relying only on herself. If she stuck to that—her standard operating procedure—she would be fine and dandy.

"Okay." She nodded with satisfaction and opened the refrigerator door, disappointment growing as the situation became clear. "Crash and burn."

There wasn't much in the way of edible, nutritious food. Ketchup. Mustard. Mayo. Diet soda. Grapes that were well on their way to spontaneous fermentation. She'd been at Nathan's house, where provisions that she didn't have to hunt and gather were plentiful. Note to self: Go to the grocery store. And while you're at it, she thought, look for an antidote to pining for peanut butter and banana sandwiches and his seventy-five-inch flat-screen TV.

She managed to find a frozen dinner and was just about to put it in the microwave when the doorbell rang. Her heart did a little skip, then sped up in a way that always signalled her expectation to see Nathan. It was proof that she'd resumed her normally scheduled life just in the nick of time. Expectations were a precursor to disappointment and heartache. She couldn't afford either.

After a stern talking-to, she walked into the living room and peeked out the window to see who was there. Her heart went back to accelerated rhythm, which was standard Nathan mode. That was acceptable because he was actually standing on the porch.

She turned the deadbolt and opened the door, ridiculously glad to see him. "Hi."

"Hi." He held up a bag. "I brought rotisserie chicken. Potatoes to bake. And salad. Are you interested? Or have you already—"

"I could kiss you—" She grabbed his arm and pulled him inside. "Not really. It's just an expression."

And that was just an excuse for the slip of the tongue. She would have wanted to kiss him even if he had nothing in his hand.

"The cupboard is bare?" he guessed.

"Pretty much."

Cindy closed the door behind him and ignored the happy little bubble expanding inside her as she led the way to the kitchen.

"What can I do?" he asked.

Just his presence was enough, but she couldn't say that. "How about setting the table?"

While he did that, she microwaved potatoes instead of the frozen dinner that probably tasted worse than the military's ready-to-eat meals.

Within ten minutes they were sitting across from each other at her small table. She looked at the whole chicken he'd neatly carved into recognizable parts.

"You should have been a surgeon," she said.

"Not my field of interest." He sliced off a piece of meat and chewed. "How was your first day back?"

"Good. Normal. Nothing much to report."

"That's a relief."

She glanced up at him. "Were you worried? Is that why you stopped by?"

He shrugged. "I wanted to check up on you. And the baby. Just make sure everything was okay."

"It was nice of you to bring food." It was nice, period, but she kept that to herself. She took a bite and sighed with pleasure. "I can't believe how good this tastes."

"You must be hungry." He frowned. "Did you eat lunch today?"

"As a matter of fact I did. With Annie Daniels."

He looked surprised. "Really?"

"I know. Shocked the heck out of me, too, when she came in the cafeteria and sat down at my table."

"She's good people," he said.

"Agreed. She advised me to put my energy into taking care of me and the baby. And I quote, 'to hell with the rest of the crap.'" There was no point in mentioning what his partner had said about the weird and wonderful chemistry between men and women.

He grinned. "Gotta love Annie."

Speaking of chemistry, Cindy felt a ridiculous tug of jealousy. She wasn't proud of it, but that didn't change the feeling. And there was no reason for it. Nathan's medical partner was married. The couple was looking into having children. Unlike them, she and Nathan weren't a couple, but they were definitely having a child. And they hadn't discussed any legalities or logistics. Maybe it was time to dip a toe into that water.

"So, did your mother tell you she wants to turn your home office into a nursery?"

He looked up quickly. "What?"

"Yeah. She showed me sketches for a wall mural—generic baby, boy and girl themes. She's going to let you make the final decision."

"Big of her," he mumbled, "what with me paying the mortgage and all."

"They're really good, the sketches, I mean." She met his gaze. "She claimed it's not talent, but practice because she had lots of time on her hands after your dad left."

"She was only deserted once. I got it twice." He put down his fork. "Three times if you count getting uprooted from home against my will and dumped in boarding school."

"Oh, my—" Cindy didn't think. She just needed to touch him. Reaching across the table, she put her hand on his arm. The warm strength there was vivid contrast to the stark vulnerability in his expression. "How old were you?"

"Eight or nine."

"Oh, Nathan—how awful. That's why you didn't have a childhood."

He shrugged but didn't slide his arm away from her touch. "I got used to it."

"Still—"

"It was hard. Eventually I realized they did me a favor. I made friends. Learned to be self-reliant. Independent. I got good grades and became a doctor."

He learned about everything but love. The one time he gave it a try, fate kicked him in the teeth when his wife died. No wonder he couldn't reach out now. She could hardly blame him. But it made her so sad.

"Cindy?"

"Hmm?"

"Are you all right?"

"Sure." She met his worried gaze. "Why?"

He turned his hand over and closed his fingers around hers. "You look like someone edited out the happy ending of one of your chick flicks."

In a way, someone had. But that wasn't a place she wanted to go.

"No," she said. "I was just thinking."

"Uh oh. Scary."

"I know, right?" She saw the expectant expression in his eyes and knew he was waiting for her to explain.

"What were you thinking about?"

"Life." She shrugged. "It's pretty unfair sometimes."

"How do you mean?"

"Your parents were so lucky to have you and they didn't appreciate the amazing gift of a child."

He frowned, clearly not getting her drift. "Like I said, I'm okay. Boarding school didn't really turn me to the dark side or anything."

"Right. I was actually thinking about Annie. She told me about losing her baby. And not being able to have another one. That had to be devastating."

"Yeah. It sucks. She really wants kids."

"That's what I mean. Your parents had a brilliant, hand-some child—"

"Thank you." His mouth curved up as humor pushed the darkness from his expression.

"That was simply the truth and not a comment made to inflate your already bloated ego." She smiled. "But why does that happen? Your parents didn't appreciate the gift. And someone like Annie who would embrace the whole exciting and magical experience can't have it."

"She's looking at surrogacy or adoption," he said.

"That's what she told me." Then a thought occurred to her. "Maybe that's the bigger plan."

"What?" His gaze never wavered as he threaded his fingers with hers instead of releasing her hand.

Tingles danced through her, making it difficult to form a coherent thought. But she hunkered down and forced herself to concentrate. "There are so many children in this world who don't have homes and parents. Maybe she's meant to be a mom to a baby who doesn't have one."

"That's a very rose-colored-glasses take on a lousy situation."

"I guess I'm just a rose-colored-glasses kind of gal," she said. "It beats doom and gloom."

"And I don't believe in fate, destiny and a grand plan. Give me science, data. Hard evidence. I'll take that over mysticism and conjecture any day of the week."

"Don't you ever make a guess in practicing medicine?" she asked.

"It's an *educated* guess, based on scientific studies and verification."

He'd said up front that he put facts over love, but part of her had been hoping it wasn't true. Now she knew he really needed to see and touch something to know it was real. Part of her wanted to shake some sense into him. The other part finally understood why he felt that way. And again sadness overwhelmed her.

His career was all about giving life a fighting chance, but in his life he wouldn't give love a chance. To her, that wasn't really living.

Cindy had grown up surrounded by love. She'd seen her parents pack a whole lot of living into life even when a cancer diagnosis cut their time together short. Her father had tenderly and with dedicated devotion nursed his wife until she took her last breath.

That's the kind of love she wanted.

It meant her problem was the exact opposite of Nathan's. She'd seen how good love could be and tended to jump into a relationship with both feet. But her eyes were wide open now. No matter how good it felt to have Nathan watching over her, she needed to resist her pattern. The jerk who'd put her in debt had just stolen her money and trust.

With Nathan, going all in could be a bigger disaster. Repairing bad credit was a walk in the park compared to the impossibility of putting a broken heart back together.

Chapter Twelve

Nathan watched the taillights of Cindy's aging compact brighten as she braked for the light on Water Street and Lake Mead Boulevard. Her right signal light went on and when traffic permitted, she made the turn. He did the same when it was safe to do so. Just as he'd been doing for weeks now. He knew the way to her house like the back of his hand.

They'd fallen into this routine since she'd gone back to work after the pregnancy scare. He either followed her home or, if he was tied up with a patient, he stopped by later when he was free. The official excuse, if anyone asked, was to make sure she was okay. But no one asked because he was careful not to draw attention to her, as she'd requested.

Privately, on some level, he knew this time was the best part of his day and he looked forward to it. If anyone demanded an explanation, he would swear on a stack of Bibles that this was about avoiding his mother.

Shirley was in a holding pattern, too. For some reason she hadn't returned to her condo in LA and was sticking around longer than usual. She claimed it was about her astrology class and the genius teacher who was tutoring her about the alignment of stars and planets. But Nathan suspected it had more to do with Cindy and the baby. Apparently making excuses to cover a certain behavior was a Steele family trait.

But the fact was, he wasn't the only Steele who dropped in on Cindy. Originally skeptical of her motives, Shirley had stopped by on the pretext of getting to know the woman who would be the mother of her first grandchild. She was nothing if not cynical and eventually had been won over. His baby mama's sweet nature had made his mother a fan.

That didn't run in the family. He was simply doing his duty.

He parked at the curb in front of her house just as she stepped out of her car. Obviously she'd made it just fine and he could have waved and driven away. But that's not what he did. After exiting the driver's side, he met her and together they walked to the front door.

"Want to come in for dinner?" she asked.

"What's on the menu?" It didn't really matter because he wasn't planning to leave even if she was serving slop.

"Tacos. I put a chuck roast in the crock pot before leaving for work this morning. It should be stringy by now. All I have to do is assemble everything else."

"I'll give you a hand."

"Thanks."

The porch light turned the honey color of her hair into a halo and the smile on her lips was nearly painful in its sweetness and beauty. Who died and made him a poet? The poetic turn of his thoughts made him feel sheepish. Fortunately she wasn't a mind reader.

After opening the door, she flipped on the living room light and started inside. She stopped so suddenly that he ran into her. Either that or he was following too closely, just to stay within arm's reach of her warmth. Either way the result was the same. He wanted to wrap his arms around her.

"Sorry," he mumbled.

That was pretty much a lie. The only thing he was sorry about was that the contact was too brief. He wanted to pull her against him while he breathed in the fresh, floral fragrance of her hair. He wouldn't have to lower his head all that much to touch his mouth to her neck.

"I forgot to get the mail," she said, starting to move around him.

"I'll get it."

"That's okay, I'll just run back out."

"No running. Let me."

"Okay. Thanks."

A few minutes outside to regroup was a good idea. It was summer and still over a hundred degrees, even though the sun would be going down soon. But a brief break was just the prescription to remind himself of all the reasons why kissing her neck was not the smartest move to make.

He walked out to the mailbox at the curb. Before reaching inside, he took a deep breath. She'd accepted his original dinner invitation just to get him off her back and now they were having a baby. Those were the facts. It was harder to quantify anything else. This compulsion to see her every night, to make sure she was okay, were actions firmly under the responsibility umbrella, but it didn't quite wash. Fortunately he didn't have to figure it out today.

He opened the door on her mailbox that looked like a miniature Quonset hut, then reached inside. There was quite a stack of envelopes, most of them official-looking and not of the junk mail variety. As he walked back to the front door, bright rays of light from the setting sun hit him full in the face until Cindy's house blocked it out. Sort of reminded him how she obstructed rational thought.

Inside, the coolness from the air conditioner felt good. He dropped her mail on the cedar chest coffee table, then joined her in the kitchen. She'd changed into white shorts and a black tank top. Her feet were bare and the sexy, domestic picture she made just cutting up lettuce and to- mato made him want to swallow his tongue. Heat slammed through him as though his time-out to regroup had never happened.

"What can I do?" He hoped his tone didn't sound as pathetic as it felt. Guidance would definitely be in order, but it probably needed to come from a shrink.

She glanced over her shoulder and smiled. "The usual—

"Set the table," he finished along with her.

Five minutes later they were sitting across from each other with taco shells, meat, beans, cheese, lettuce and tomatoes in containers between them. Nathan fixed one with everything, then wolfed it down, surprised at how hungry he was. Cindy did the same, but she ate at a more ladylike pace.

He needed to distract himself from watching her mouth. Food wasn't all he was hungry for, but it was all he'd let himself have.

"So, it's about time you gave me another shopping list," he said. "There must be some things you need."

She wiped her mouth with a napkin. "You really don't have to do my shopping, Nathan. I'm well past the first trimester and the doctor says there's no reason to believe I'll have any more problems."

"Good to know. And I intend to keep it that way."

"By shopping for me?"

If only that's all it would take to ensure that the rest of her pregnancy was healthy. "That and carrying it all. You can't be too careful."

Her eyes gleamed with mischief. "Okay, burly boy. What if I told you there was a sale on canned vegetables and I bought a case? *And* carried it in the house without assistance?"

One of his eyebrows went up. "Burly boy?"

"That would be you."

"I've been called science geek and math nerd, but never burly boy."

She laughed, such a merry and bright sound that it lighted a dark place deep inside him and took away some of the shadows.

"I appreciate you helping out," she said, "but it's really not necessary."

"Maybe not." But he remembered what Annie had said about not letting her physically exert herself. And that was before she'd had a problem. "Either make me a new list or I'll go by the old one."

"No, please, anything but that." Her expression was rueful. "I have enough paper towels to clean up a toxic waste dump. If I have to store more, there won't be any room for me."

He barely held back the words on the tip of his tongue, which were to the effect that she should move back in with him. Instead he said, "I have one word. *List.*"

She held up her hands in surrender. "Okay. You win."

"That works for me."

When they'd both finished eating, he helped her put the

leftovers away and clean up the dishes. It was time for him to go and the shadows that had disappeared a little while ago were creeping back. He was trying to figure out how to put off leaving when she gave him a way.

"Would you like some coffee?"

"Yeah," he said. "I would. But I'll make it. You go sit in the living room and put your feet up. That's an order."

She must have been tired because there was no argument. Just a sassy salute. After all these weeks he knew his way around her tiny kitchen and fixed himself a cup of instant coffee, then joined her in the other room. Not only were her feet still on the floor, she was staring at the stack of mail and frowning.

He set down his mug on the cedar chest, then lowered himself to the sofa beside her. "I'm not used to having my orders disobeyed."

"Hmm?" She glanced at him.

"Your feet aren't up."

This time when she smiled there was sadness around the edges. "You sound like my dad."

He preferred *burly boy*. "Why?"

"I was about nine when my mom was pregnant with my brother. So I remember a lot. My dad would make her sit down and then he rubbed her feet." There was a suspicious brightness in her eyes when she looked at him.

"What's wrong, Cindy?"

"They'd be so disappointed in me." She flicked the stack of mail, and it toppled to the floor on the other side of the chest. "My bills rival the national debt. And that's not what they would have wanted. I've made some really bad choices."

Nathan was in the business of fixing things and badly wanted to now. But this wasn't a science-based problem with formulas and solutions. Mostly he couldn't stand to see her upset. He didn't know how to fix what was wrong, but he had to try.

"Everyone has done something they'd like to take back." For him it would be asking Felicia to marry him. A man who didn't believe in love had no business making promises he couldn't keep. "It's not your fault the guy conned you. And if your mother and father were here they'd tell you the same thing. It's a parent's duty to make sure their kids can function independently. Mine did an exemplary job on that score," he said wryly. The rest of it was a dismal failure, but that wasn't pertinent to this conversation. "The point is that you didn't give up. You didn't ask for help. You simply picked up the pieces and moved on. You're putting your brother through college and working to pay your bills. It seems to me that your parents would be extraordinarily proud of you."

"Thanks for that, Nathan," she whispered.

"You're welcome." He didn't usually make speeches and was disconcerted that he'd done it now. "Okay, moving on. Put your feet in my lap."

"What?"

"Just do it. That's an order. I'm going to take care of you."

Without another word, she swung her legs onto his thighs and leaned back against the arm of the love seat. He took one of her slender ankles in his hand and with the other he pressed a thumb into the arch of her foot.

"How does that feel?"

"Heavenly."

The sound that came from her throat was somewhere between a moan and a groan, as if she were in the throes of passion. In a nanosecond, the blood drained from his head and raced south of his belt.

"Good." He could only manage the single word and it

came out more rasp than anything else. The wanting was getting worse every day, proof that his character was in serious trouble.

"Now I know why my mom liked this so much." When she met his gaze, her eyes were filled with tears again. "I w-wish they were here to see their grandchild—"

Cindy stopped, unable to get any more words past the lump in her throat. She hated the pregnancy hormones that made her so emotional. But she had a feeling this would have gotten to her even if she wasn't having a baby. This gesture reminded her of the loving relationship her parents had. The way her father had cared for her mother all through their marriage, right up until the day she'd died.

And that's when the tears went rolling down her cheeks and she put her hands over her face.

"What is it?" Nathan's deep voice was laced with concern.

"I'm pregnant," she managed to say.

"Not a newsflash." Now there was just a hint of humor in his tone. "Why are you crying? Although it makes no sense to me, don't women sometimes cry when they're happy? Is it possible this is one of those times?"

How could she tell him that he was the problem? That she wanted what her parents had and she wanted it from him. Whatever his hang-ups were, he was still a good man. He hadn't disappeared as expected; he'd been there from the moment she'd told him about the baby. How could he understand that it wasn't enough, would never be enough?

She brushed at the moisture on her cheeks and tried to smile with mixed results. "You got me. Happy tears."

His expression was skeptical. "Really?"

"Yeah." But another tear leaked out. "I think I n-need to be alone."

She pulled her legs off his thighs and straightened away

from the sofa arm, turning beside him to put her feet on the floor. Before she could stand up, he put one arm behind her back and the other beneath her legs, then scooped her into his arms and onto his lap.

"Not so fast."

"Please—I feel so silly."

"And I hate to see you cry. So if there's anything I can do to fix it, I'm going to. Now talk to me."

Through a shimmery blur of tears she looked at him, his face just inches from her own. Concern was etched in his eyes and there was tension in his lean jaw. The steady determination in his gaze was proof that he was dead serious about making it better. The utter sweetness of the gesture brought on a fresh wave of waterworks.

"Sorry. I just can't help it. I'm in hormone hell."

When he gathered her into his arms, she buried her face against his neck.

"I can't fix hormones. That's chemistry. Your body's taking care of the baby."

The words were a gentle, reassuring whisper as his breath stirred her hair. Shivers danced down her neck and put a hitch in her breathing. Body chemistry was going on, but suddenly this had nothing to do with the baby and everything to do with repeating the act that had created it in the first place.

When she lifted her head, their gazes collided and Cindy saw in his eyes a yearning that mirrored her own. It wasn't clear if he moved first or she did, but suddenly their mouths were locked together in a hungry fusing of mutual need.

She slid her arms around his neck and pressed against the solid wall of his chest. Breasts sensitive from pregnancy tingled from the contact and she yearned to know how it would feel without clothes blocking the sensation. Nathan's hands alternately rubbed up her back and curved around her waist, his thumbs skimming the undersides of her breasts. He kissed and nipped her mouth and chin, cheek and jaw.

When he traced her lips with his tongue, she opened her mouth to him, eagerly inviting him inside. He entered and took over, boldly laying a claim that she gratefully turned over to him. She welcomed the invasion, the invitation into the dark and dangerous. There was no fear or hesitation as her tongue dueled with his. The sound of his quickened breathing was like an echo of thunder announcing the coming storm. And she welcomed that, too.

With the flat of her hand she touched his broad shoulders and strong back, savoring the masculine feel of him. She leaned back against his arm and tried to tug him down on the love seat.

"No—"

Every part of her cried out in protest at being denied the pleasure his body had promised.

She forced out words in spite of her labored breathing. "But I thought you wanted—"

He nodded. "Not here. This time it's going to be good."

"Last time was pretty amazing." She could tease now that she knew he hadn't changed his mind.

"Not what I meant. I want to do it right." He put a finger on her mouth to shut off the smart-ass comment he knew was coming. "This time I want it right, with you in bed."

Her heart melted. She could feel the warmth trickling through her.

She smiled. "Why didn't I think of that?"

"Because I have the superior IQ and skills to—"

This time she silenced him with a quick kiss before saying, "That was a rhetorical question."

"I'll show you rhetorical." His voice was a sexy growl as he stood with her in his arms.

Her heart did that melty thing again and she barely held in a sigh. "You should put me down before you hurt yourself."

He settled her more firmly in his arms as he said, "You know, the density of peanut butter and banana is definitely evident."

"Watch it, buster."

"You hardly weigh anything," he said, already moving down the hall toward her bedroom.

"Much more politically correct," she approved.

When he stopped beside her bed, he gently set her on her feet next to it. "Someone was in a hurry this morning."

She glanced over her shoulder at the jumble of sea foam green sheets, blanket and floral-patterned quilt on the un-made, queen-size bed. "Are you going to dock my allow-ance for not completing my chores?"

"Actually I was thinking more in terms of a bonus for exemplary time-management skills. Now I don't have to unmake the bed."

The teasing in his eyes mixed with something bright and hot that set her skin on fire. She slid her hands up underneath his black T-shirt and settled her palms on his bare flesh. He grabbed the hem and pulled it off in one fast, fluid, ever-so-manly motion.

Cindy did the same with her tank top before he reached behind her and unhooked her bra. She felt it release and he took the straps, sliding them down her arms. The scrap of lingerie fell to the floor between them.

The snap on her shorts was already undone, a conces-sion to her expanding waistline. When Nathan noticed, a slow sexy smile curved up the corners of his mouth. He unzipped her pants and she pushed them over her hips and stepped out. Nathan settled his palm on her belly, now rounding with the baby bump.

His hand was warm and all he said was, "Wow."

"Yeah, huh? Overnight I just got fat—"

"No." He shook his head. "It's perfectly natural. And you look incredibly beautiful."

"My fragile ego chooses to believe you even though that's a bald-faced lie."

"I've never meant anything more. You're beautiful, Cindy. So beautiful…"

His voice trailed off as he leaned down and settled his mouth on hers. It was the barest brush of his lips, but still the breath backed up in her chest. That kiss was the only place their bodies touched and yet it was like a flashpoint, sending heat burning back and forth between them. He removed his shorts and boxers and was now magnificently naked.

He pulled back and eyed her panties. "One of us is over-dressed."

She looked at him, so ready that her heart lurched and her legs felt weak. "And one of us is an overachiever."

He laughed before backing her up against the mattress, then gently lowering her to the cool sheets. He slid one finger beneath the waistband of her underwear and into her waiting warmth. She sucked in air even as she wiggled out of the last of her clothes.

Anticipation knotted inside her as he brushed his thumb across the bundle of nerve endings at her center. The touch was driving her closer to the edge, making her crazy with wanting. She nearly whimpered when he stopped.

Before she could protest, he rolled on top of her and nudged her thighs apart. Taking most of his weight on his elbows, he slipped inside her and she felt him catch his breath at the same time hers caught. Then he stroked in and out, slowly building the storm inside her until she was swamped with sensation.

He drove her crazy, took her to the top of the swell, then groaned as they both rode the wave over the crest and down, drowning in the pleasure that washed through them.

Nathan held her until the quaking stopped and she could breathe again. She expected him to let her go then, but he didn't. With a satisfied sigh, he gathered her closer and she rested her palm on his chest. Feeling the strong and steady beat of his heart, hope swelled inside her.

He hadn't said the words, but maybe, just maybe he was beginning to feel something warm and deep for her. The tenderest of emotions flooded her heart and this wasn't about hormones. He'd been right about taking her to the bedroom and he didn't really understand how much.

Her parents had spent their lives together in this house, this room. They'd raised two children, lived, argued, made up and loved here. She felt their presence, the two loving spirits watching over her, and knew they weren't disappointed. Just the opposite.

The sensation made her believe in possibilities. Nathan was a show-don't-tell kind of guy. The fact was that he'd shown her with his hands, mouth and body that he was tender and protective. It was just possible that was his way of showing what was in his heart. Wasn't it possible that the affectionate and adoring spirit of love that permeated this place might have just rubbed off on him?

Maybe he actually *could* love her.

Chapter Thirteen

Nathan put his hand on Cindy's arm to stop her from getting out of the car. "You can't hide your pregnancy much longer."

"I know."

Shadows drifted through her eyes and he hated himself for putting them there. He'd picked her up and brought her to Dr. Hamilton's office for her ultrasound. It was hard to believe, but she was already in her fifth month of pregnancy. Loose-fitting tops and big sweaters with excuses about the air-conditioning making her cold weren't going to conceal her condition for much longer.

The days and weeks had turned into months that passed in a blur. His mother was still in his guest house, which was probably a world record, but he didn't want to know why and she didn't say. Nathan had enough trouble figuring out what this thing was with Cindy.

He saw her nearly every day, but his story for the pattern

of behavior was wearing thin. After the problem in the first few weeks, the pregnancy had been textbook normal. How much longer could he claim that he was checking up on her because of the baby? Or making sure she ate right for the baby?

He sure hadn't slept with her again because of the baby.

That had only confused the issue more, so he'd been careful not to make the mistake again. His reaction to her was so powerful, it was entirely possible that he couldn't do without her. And he would never let himself depend on anyone that completely.

There was only one problem with abstinence. Wanting her again was eating him up inside. They didn't live together, but they might as well. Either he was at her place or she was at his. And the hell of it was that when he wasn't with her, he wanted to be. He worried about her and couldn't completely blame that on the fact that she was pregnant with his child.

Her hand was resting on the car's console between them and he covered it with his own. "Have you thought about what you're going to say to people?"

"You don't think they'll swallow the story of too many cheeseburgers and fries?"

He remembered her saying she was fat the night he'd taken her to bed. It had ticked him off more than a little. The sight of her—honey-blond hair tumbled around her face, the gentle swell of her belly that was his baby growing inside her—was the most profoundly beautiful thing he'd ever seen. And sexy as hell. If he'd had a prayer of not sleeping with her, it disappeared in that second.

Nathan shook his head. "No one will believe you're getting fat."

She smiled a smile that was mischievous around the

edges. "The speculation will drive them crazy. Is she or isn't she?"

By "them" he knew she meant the nurses at the hospital who'd given her a hard time. And that was the reason he'd brought this up in the first place. When the news broke, he didn't want Cindy stressed out by anything.

He raised an eyebrow. "This is a side of you that I've never seen before."

"What?"

"Kind of wicked."

"Gotta take the victories where you find 'em." She shrugged. "If those witches in the NICU want to know for sure, they'll actually have to speak to me and not make snide comments behind my back."

It was frustrating that she wouldn't let him run interference to make sure no one upset her. "And you'll tell them too many cheeseburgers?"

"Maybe they'd believe I swallowed a watermelon seed."

"They're nothing if not narrow-minded, but they were smart enough to pass anatomy and physiology classes. I'm not sure that explanation would fly."

"Then I'll just let them make their own assumptions."

"And when they want to know who the father is?" he asked.

"Immaculate conception?"

It was definitely conception, but nothing about it had been immaculate. Sex had been messy, sweaty, spontaneous, passionate and completely mind-blowing. Cindy made him feel that way again every time he was with her.

He took a breath to steady his elevated pulse. "No one will go for that any more than the fruit story."

She tilted her head and studied him closely. "Are you afraid that I'll rat you out, Doctor?"

"What?"

"Don't worry. I won't spill your secret. No one will know you've been slumming with the housekeeper."

"You may or may not be kidding, but stop right there." This could be pregnancy hormones or just her personal peeve but he wasn't letting it go. "I've been ready to support you from day one. I don't give a damn what anyone says. Apparently that's your thing. You told me to back off—"

"I know." She held up a hand. "You're right. I'm sorry. That was completely unfair. I guess you just caught me off guard when you pointed out that very soon it will be obvious that I'm pregnant."

"I apologize—"

"No. You're right. It's crossed my mind, but I've been burying my head in the sand."

"You know what happens then, right?" he asked.

She met his gaze and the corners of her full mouth curved up. "I leave my backside exposed?"

"Pretty much."

"What do you think I should say?" she asked seriously.

"Probably that you don't believe—"

"Whoa," she interrupted, glancing at her wristwatch. "We're late for the ultrasound. That's pretty bad when we've been sitting here in the parking lot for fifteen minutes."

"Let's go."

It was a conversation they needed to have but not in an obstetrician's waiting room full of women. The reality was that the doctor would probably be running late and wouldn't notice they were a few minutes behind schedule.

As they walked through the parking lot and the medical building's desert landscaped courtyard, Nathan settled his palm at the small of Cindy's back. He'd almost taken her hand, an intimate, automatic gesture that came out of nowhere.

Intimate gestures didn't come automatically to him.

That was one of the things his wife had called him out on. During an ugly scene, she'd accused him of being a clone of his father. Then she'd walked out on him just like everyone else.

The interior of Rebecca Hamilton's office was dim and cool after the heat outside. Summer was almost over, but the Las Vegas Valley wouldn't give up its warm days for a while yet. He remembered Cindy's remark about not having to go through being big as a battleship while it was hot. Now she was big enough to have an ultrasound.

She signed in at the reception desk, but before they could take a seat, the back office door opened.

The dark-haired young woman wore blue scrubs and held a chart in her hands. "Cindy Elliott?"

"Here," she answered, raising her hand as if someone were taking attendance.

"Come on back."

"I feel like a game show contestant," she confessed nervously.

When he started to sit down, the office assistant said, "Your husband can come with you if you'd like."

Cindy looked at him and faltered. He could almost read her mind. Should she set the record straight about their relationship? Let the error ride? Or was she hesitating about whether to invite him into the experience?

Cindy looked at him. "I'd like you to be there."

"Okay."

Her reasoning might have been about nerves, even though she'd already had the test once. She knew the procedure was noninvasive. This time he wanted to be in the room with her, but he hadn't pushed. There were privacy laws in place and because they weren't married, any of her medical information wouldn't automatically be revealed to him without Cindy's permission.

He understood the need for rules, and it had never bothered him before. But it did now. He had a personal interest; this was his baby. That lame excuse again. It was the best he could do.

After the assistant weighed Cindy and took her blood pressure, she got her settled on an exam table with the ultrasound machine beside it. Nathan pulled up a chair and prepared for a lengthy wait. But moments later the doctor walked in.

"Hi, Cindy." She looked at him. "Nathan. How are you?"

"Fine."

"Congratulations, by the way."

"Thanks."

The doctor looked at him. "Are you ready to meet your baby for the first time?"

"Yes," he said, as excitement rippled through him.

Cindy smiled radiantly at him and that sent a different sort of ripple through his system.

The doctor pulled down the sheet and lifted Cindy's shirt to squirt warm gel on her gently rounded belly. She moved the transducer and turned dials on the machine to improve resolution and get optimum views.

And then he could see the image. That was his baby! He'd known the fetus was real, but now he really understood what Rebecca had meant about meeting his child. He'd never felt anything like this and was moved beyond words.

"See the pulsing, Cindy?" Rebecca pointed to the screen. "That's your baby's heart. It looks strong. Normal. Here are the arms and legs."

"Oh, my goodness," Cindy breathed. "Nathan, do you see?"

"Yeah."

The doctor glanced at them. "Do you want to know your baby's sex?"

"Yes."

They both said it at the same time even though the topic had never come up for discussion. The fact they agreed sent a warm feeling through him.

"Are you sure you want to know?" he asked.

"Very sure." Cindy grinned. "Then Shirley can get started on the mural."

He'd forgotten about that, but it would explain why his mom was sticking around. Still, it was out of character for her to be there for a kid, even if it was her first grandchild.

"Okay," he said to the doc. "We're in total agreement. If you can get a good view."

She studied the screen for a while. Frustrated she said, "Move your leg, little one." A few moments later she smiled. "We have a boy."

Without thinking Nathan took Cindy's hand and squeezed gently. He stared hard at his son moving in her womb. A powerful feeling of protectiveness moved through him. They were having a boy, a tiny perfect son who would need them to be there for him. Both of them. Together.

Nathan had no blueprint for successful parenting. His childhood had pretty much sucked. But he'd had one thing his son didn't. A father and mother who were legally married when he was born.

That was something easily fixed.

"So, thanks for dinner." Cindy looked up at Nathan, tall and handsome in the moonlight, and wished he would kiss her.

She was standing on her front porch, so close to him the heat from his body warmed her skin. After the ultrasound he'd taken her to celebrate at Capriotti's where he showed off the ultrasound picture of his son. Now they were awfully close to the exact spot where their son had been conceived.

She wanted a repeat of that impulsive, explosive, out-of-control sex. Or even sweet, slow bedroom sex. Any sex, really, because they'd been drifting along in limbo and she needed a sign that there was reason to hope he could care as much for her as she did for him.

Nathan rubbed a hand across the back of his neck. "Would you mind if I came in? There's something I'd like to talk to you about."

Talk didn't really thrill her. He was looking very serious about something and that was never a good thing. She could think of a much better use for their mouths than conversation. But, again, hope deflated like a leaky balloon because his mood was leaning more toward serious than sexy. She needed to concentrate on the baby.

A boy!

Maybe a rough-and-tumble little guy. Or possibly a brilliant, quiet heartbreaker like his father.

"I'm awfully tired, Nathan. It's been a big day. Exciting," she added, "But really exhausting."

"What I have to say is pretty important. I promise it won't take long," he said. "There's just something I'd like to settle between us."

Cindy studied him and would swear he actually looked a little nervous. It was a side to him she'd never seen. He'd been concerned when the doctor put her on bed rest, but this was different. The always unflappable Dr. Nathan Steele actually looked—flappable.

"Okay." She fit her key into the lock, then opened the door. "Come in."

"Thanks."

She set her purse on the cedar chest. "Do you want something to drink?"

"No."

Studying the solemn expression on his face, she asked, "Is this a standing-up sort of conversation, or something I should sit down for?"

"That depends."

"On what?"

"How surprised you're going to be."

He'd said they needed to settle something, which probably meant this was about the baby. His reaction to the ultrasound had been clear to anyone within visual range of his face. Quite literally he'd been beaming. Such a guy, pleased this was a boy child to carry on his name.

His name?

She suddenly went cold all over. "You want to take the baby away from me?" Another thought struck her, and she didn't have the financial resources to fight him. "You're going to sue me for custody?"

"No." He looked horrified. "God, no."

She'd been holding her breath and finally let it out. "Okay. Sorry. Sometimes I go to the bad place."

"That's an understatement. You don't even slow down for stop signs when you go there."

"It's easier that way." She shrugged. "Get the very worst out of the way and the rest isn't so bad."

He ran his fingers through his hair. "Well, I'm sort of hoping this isn't something even in the same neighborhood with the bad place."

She walked over to the love seat and sat. "Maybe this is

a sit-down talk after all. If nothing else, I can take a load off while you get to the point."

"I think you should marry me."

She blinked up at him. "What did you say?"

"We need to get married."

"That's what I thought you said. Way to get to the point."

Cindy knew she'd chosen wisely in sitting down. The shock of his point would have dropped her like a stone.

Married?

He wanted to marry her? Happiness expanded inside her. This was something she hadn't dared to let herself hope for.

His gaze never left hers as the silence grew. Finally he said, "Please say something. What are you thinking?"

"Wow. I'm thinking a proposal, really?"

"Yes, really." He sat on the cedar chest in front of her. "Seeing our baby really put things in perspective for me."

"Such as?" She really wanted him to touch her. When a guy proposed marriage, didn't he at least take her hand?

"A kid needs a mother and father."

"Check." She pointed to herself, then him. "Both present and accounted for."

"And a stable environment. That means both parents under the same roof."

"We've kind of been doing that already."

"I don't want 'kind of.' I think we need to officially be under the same roof to make a family."

Why did he want to get married now? Something didn't feel right.

"This is important to you?" she asked.

"It is. I never want my son to feel different, out-of-step, that he doesn't fit—"

"Because his parents aren't legally married?"

"Yes," he said, as if she'd come up with the elusive answer to the riddle of the day.

He'd listed logical reasons to take the step, but not one of them was about loving her. He'd said "We need to get married," not "I want to marry you."

Silence stretched to the breaking point between them before he finally said again, "Please say something. Tell me what you're thinking."

"Honestly?"

"That would be good."

Cindy blew out a long breath. "Because we both know life isn't a romantic comedy and you just asked me to marry you, I'm honestly wondering why."

"I told you why," he protested.

"You listed legal and logistical reasons, but not one of them was the most important one."

"I don't understand."

The endearingly clueless expression on his face tugged at her heart. "Then I'll explain it to you."

"Please."

"During our very first conversation you told me that you don't believe in something if you can't see or touch it."

"I remember. You're talking about love." His expression shuttered.

"Yes." She gripped her hands together in her lap. "But your mother told me you and your wife were completely in love. That you were inconsolable when she died and blamed yourself. To me, that doesn't sound like a man who doesn't believe love exists."

"The only part of what my mother said that's true is I do blame myself for everything that went wrong." His voice was harsh and cold.

"Meaning what?"

"I liked and respected my wife. That should have been enough, but it wasn't. She left me." He ran his fingers through his hair. "In all fairness, I was never there for her. Work always came first."

That was hard to believe. He'd been there for her, Cindy, from the beginning. Asking for her phone number. Persistently. Then when she found out she was pregnant, he'd had to wear down her resistance because she kept waiting for him to not be there. When had she started to trust him? It was all a blur, but she realized she did have faith that he wouldn't run out on her. But that was only now because she and the baby were one.

"Shirley didn't say anything about that," she accused.

"Because she doesn't know. You may have noticed that Shirley and I don't really communicate all that much."

"But still… That was a life-changing event in your life. You're her son."

"There was no point. Felicia and I had just separated when she was killed in the accident. Shirley didn't need to know we were getting a divorce." Sadness and anger fused together in his grim expression. "If I'd been capable of loving her the way she deserved to be loved, she would still be alive."

So he hadn't been in love. She'd truly thought he was capable of the emotion because he'd been married. The truth made it hard to breathe.

"You don't know that things would have been different if your feelings were deeper," she said, trying to be rational when she just wanted to fall apart.

"Yeah. I do." His mind was made up about that. "I missed my best friend, but she was never the love of my life. I don't even know what that means."

Because he'd never seen what love looked like. Cindy knew something else, too. His greatest strength was also his biggest flaw. Scrupulous honesty. He'd told her straight up that he didn't believe in love and was now proving it wasn't a lie.

But Cindy had been lying to herself.

She'd thought her heart was protected by scar tissue from her last disastrous relationship. Now she realized the foolishness of that strategy. She was the kind of person who led with her heart. And she'd always known she wanted to be someone's great love. As her trust in Nathan grew, she'd yearned for that someone to be him.

She was completely and hopelessly in love with him.

But he'd just told her that he couldn't be in love with anyone. It wasn't a good plan to propose marriage, then declare love didn't exist in your world.

"You're right about one thing," she said. "Shirley doesn't need to know the truth. And yet, as dysfunctional as your relationship is with her, you kept that information to yourself to protect her."

"Not really."

She didn't have the strength to argue with him. Holding back tears that desperately wanted release took all her energy. He'd asked to come in so they could settle this business of marriage. The least she could do was give him an answer.

"Thank you, no."

His eyes narrowed. "No what?"

"I can't marry you. But I appreciate that you're trying to do the right thing for our son."

"You don't even want to think it over?"

"There's nothing to think about. My mind is made up just as surely as yours is." She stood and walked over to the door, then opened it. "Goodbye, Nathan."

Cindy didn't think it was possible that hope had survived the beating it had just taken, but she was wrong again. Hope didn't really breathe its last until he was gone without even trying to convince her she was wrong.

After her heart cracked in two, the last sound she heard was the squeal of tires as he drove away.

Chapter Fourteen

"Damn these pregnancy hormones—" Cindy sniffled as she set a single place at the table.

It always seemed so small when Nathan sat across from her. Now it felt big enough to land a jumbo jet, and had for the last week. That's how long it had been since the night he'd proposed. A short time and yet being alone made it feel like forever.

She'd seen him briefly at work but hadn't talked to him. And every night, right about the time he usually rang her doorbell, the tears started when no one came.

"Stop it," she ordered herself.

She was preparing to cut up vegetables for a salad and actually being able to see would be good. She needed all her fingers. An appetite would come in handy, too, but that had been missing for the past seven days.

Maybe turning him down had been a mistake. She might be in love by herself, but at least she wouldn't be alone.

"That didn't work out so well for Felicia. Or his mother." Now she was talking to herself.

She'd existed in a world where she desperately missed Nathan's warmth, humor and caring, but in her heart she knew it was the right thing. Alone was better than watching the man you loved not love you back. But she had to admit that walking by herself on the high road didn't make her feel less lonely.

She sprinkled extra-virgin olive oil and balsamic vinegar on the lettuce, tomato, cucumber and avocado in her salad bowl. Then she put in some cold diced chicken and grated cheddar cheese and placed it on the table. After adding ice to a glass, she was filling it with filtered water from the refrigerator when the doorbell rang.

Her hand jerked and water sloshed over her wrist. "Nathan?" she whispered.

She ran to the front door and peeked out the window, reminded once again how incredibly cruel hope could be. One minute on top of the world, anticipating what you wanted more than anything else. The next you were lower than you'd ever been before. There was a Steele standing outside, but it was not Nathan.

Cindy unlocked the deadbolt and opened the door. "Hi, Shirley."

"Cindy." She looked closer. "Are you all right?"

No. But she would be. When her eyes stopped feeling ten sizes too small from crying.

"I'm fine. But this isn't a very good time for me. It hasn't been a good week."

"Tell me about it." She looked upset. "This won't take long, but I really need to talk to you. It's about Nathan."

"Is he all right?" Cindy opened the door wider and let the other woman walk inside.

"He's not hurt." Shirley turned when the door closed. "At least not physically, if that's what you mean."

"What a relief." She couldn't stand the thought of anything happening to him. "I was just going to eat a salad. Can I make something for you?"

"No, thanks. I've had dinner. But you need to eat. Would you mind if I kept you company?"

"Okay." Although she didn't think her company would be very good, to talk to an actual person would be a welcome change from talking to herself. "I'd like that."

Shirley sat across the table from her in the chair Nathan usually occupied. "That's a nutritious dinner."

"I'm trying to eat healthy for the little guy."

"A boy?"

"Yes." Cindy smiled before noticing the look of awe, then stark and genuine surprise on the other woman's face. "Nathan didn't tell you."

"No."

"We found out last week at the doctor's appointment. She did an ultrasound."

The same day Nathan proposed so the son he'd just found out about wouldn't ever feel bad because his parents weren't married. There was no way to explain to him that saying "I do" was not an inoculation against dysfunctional. The queen of screwed-up relationships was sitting right across from her.

"I can't believe he didn't say anything." Shirley slid the Coach purse off her shoulder and set it on the floor beside her. "But then he hasn't been acting like himself. That's why I came to see you."

"Oh?" Cindy took a bite of salad, but couldn't taste anything.

"Yes. He's been short-tempered and moody. That's so unlike him." She linked her fingers. "I asked him about painting a bedroom for the baby and he walked away without answering. Is there something wrong with the baby?"

"No." She rested her hand protectively on her growing belly. "He's doing great."

"Thank goodness." In the next instant, the relief in her face gave way to worry. "I don't understand why he didn't tell me you were having a boy. Nathan has always been so steady, so even. There's something wrong with him. I just know it. He wouldn't talk about anything, which isn't new. But he's been acting so strangely and that is different. I was so hoping you could enlighten me."

Cindy choked down more salad before setting her fork in the bowl of half-eaten greens. She sipped some water, then took a deep breath. "Nathan proposed to me."

Shirley blinked several times, then smiled. "That's wonderful. Congratulations. I know what I said about you two being very modern and not feeling as if you had to marry for the sake of the baby. But I've gotten to know you and I think you're very good for him."

"I turned him down."

"But why?" Her smile disappeared, replaced by shock. "I don't understand. Any fool can see that you're completely in love with him."

"I am," Cindy agreed, more calmly than she felt. Especially when her heart cracked just a little bit more. "But marrying him would set a new record for foolish. It would be too painful knowing he can't love me back."

"I don't think that's true. They say a man who loved once is more likely to love again. Felicia has been gone—"

"He didn't love her." Cindy felt a pang of guilt at being the one to reveal this information. But, in spite of her faults, this woman meant well and needed to understand why there would be no wedding for her grandson's parents.

"That's not true. He was inconsolable when she died."

"Because he blamed himself for the marriage not working. When Felicia died in the accident they were separated. That being the case, he felt there was no point in revealing that to you. He understands that you were very fond of his wife."

"He was protecting me?"

"Ironic, but true," Cindy said. "Apparently Felicia walked out when she realized he didn't love her the way a husband should love his wife."

"I can't believe this." Her hazel eyes grew even wider.

"It's true." Cindy had just revealed Nathan's secret, but to make it count for something she needed to get another concern off her chest. "Nathan doesn't believe in love, Shirley. And you bear some responsibility for that."

"Me?" The older woman recoiled as if she'd been slapped. "I don't know what you mean."

"Think about it for a minute. When the going gets tough, the tough don't take art classes. But that's what you did." Cindy expected an angry, defensive reaction to her words, but there was only silence. And sadness in Shirley's expression. "You and Nathan's father had problems and neither one of you talked to him about what was going on. Neither one of you bothered to say you stopped loving each other but still loved him. You handled the situation by hiding, and that's the coping skill your little boy learned."

Shirley sighed and eyes so like her son's filled with misery and self-recrimination. "I was in no condition to be a good mother to him. You may choose to believe I'm simply making excuses for my shortcomings, but I sincerely believed that and was afraid that me being in such an emotionally damaged state, I would hurt Nathan more."

"You were wrong." Cindy couldn't hold back the words, but it wasn't her intention to hurt. Just to clear the air.

"I see that now. Obviously I've made mistakes. If I could take them back, I would do it in an instant. But if you believe nothing else, believe this—I love my son with all my heart."

Cindy could see that. "I know you do."

"This is no excuse for my behavior, but I'm not the only parent he had."

Cindy remembered Nathan saying he was abandoned by both of them and then shipped off to boarding school. Unfortunately, knowing why he was the way he was didn't flip the switch to turn on his ability to love her back.

"You're right, Shirley. His father didn't help. Nathan's whole world was falling down around him and he had no support system in place to handle what was going on."

"I wish there was something I could do to change the past." Regret shimmered in her eyes. "That's not possible. But if there's anything I can do for you, just ask."

The absolute sincerity in the other woman's expression convinced Cindy that she meant what she said. But the harm was already done and her own broken heart was collateral damage.

"Thanks, but I don't think there's anything. He won't let himself take a leap of faith that love exists and I won't tie myself to a man who can't let me be his great love. I won't settle for less. More important, my baby won't get caught up in the fallout from a mistake."

Shirley nodded but looked uneasy. "Still, don't forget that this is his child, too."

"I won't."

Cindy had thought about that a lot. He was committed to his son, so much so that he'd gone against his beliefs and proposed marriage. He cared deeply, a father's love, whether or not he thought about his feelings in those terms.

And because he cared, they would be tied together forever by this child.

"You wouldn't punish him for the sins of the parents, would you? Keep him from seeing the baby?"

"Never," Cindy vowed. "My baby deserves to know his father. Having both of us in his life is the best thing for him."

And the worst thing for her because it would hurt every time she saw him and was reminded that she was in love all by herself.

"Thank you, Cindy. You're a better mother to your son than I ever was to mine." She sighed again. "I'm sorry."

"I'm not the one you should be apologizing to."

"You're right." A determined look slid into the older woman's eyes. It was the same expression Nathan had worn when asking for Cindy's phone number. Shirley nodded resolutely, then stood. "I've taken up enough of your time."

Cindy stood and followed her to the front door. "You don't have to go."

"I have a lot to think about." She leaned over and pulled Cindy into a quick, hard hug. "You're a remarkable woman, Cindy Elliott. Honest and straightforward. My grandson is a lucky little guy to have you for his mother."

Shirley left before Cindy's tears started up again.

Sniffling, she leaned back against the door. "Damn hormones."

It was his day off, but Nathan didn't know what to do with himself. He paced his house until he wanted to put his fist through a wall. Every square inch of the five thousand plus square feet reminded him of Cindy. In fact, everything and nothing reminded him that she'd turned him down. The feelings running through him were strangely like the abandonment he'd experienced when he'd been dumped at boarding school.

Finally, he decided to channel his energy in a more productive way and drove to Mercy Medical Center. He took the elevator to the second floor and walked into the NICU. Annie was standing by the nurse's station writing in a chart. She glanced up at him, then did a double take and frowned.

After handing the chart to the charge nurse, she walked over to him and slid her hands into the pockets of her white lab coat. "It's not like you to read our schedule wrong."

"Meaning?"

"You're off today."

"I just wanted to check in on the thirty-two weeker we got yesterday."

Annie stared at him. "Buffy?"

"Please tell me that's not her legal name."

"No. That would be Alexandria Michelle Morrison. I named her Buffy—as in the vampire slayer." She tipped her head to the side. "The blank expression on your face suggests that you have no idea what I'm talking about."

"I don't."

"It's a TV show, a cultural phenomenon. The chick can kick some serious vampire ass."

"I'll take your word for it." He glanced over to where the tiny baby was sleeping. "How's Buffy doing?"

"Kicking some serious preemie problems," she said with a grin. "She's one tough little chick. Her oxygen saturation is good and the blood chemistries are within normal range. Holding her own and all signs are positive."

"Good." He looked around and noted the unit was unusually quiet. "Do you need any help?"

"You're kidding, right?"

"No." Nathan just wanted to do something, anything to keep himself from thinking about Cindy.

He'd made her a good proposition, but the cost of her counteroffer was too high. They got along great. Why mess that up by putting a label on it? That all made sense in his head, but it didn't stop him from missing her smile. The need to be with her never went away. Every night for the last week he'd left work and turned toward her house before he remembered she didn't want to see him.

"So you don't trust me to do my job?" Annie asked.

"Of course I do."

"This unscheduled drop-in says something different. It's going to start rumors about the stability of our medical practice."

"That's ridiculous. You're the best neonatologist I know. Besides me, of course."

"Of course." Her voice dripped sarcasm before she turned serious. "Then I don't get it, Nathan. Surely you have something better to do than hang around the hospital."

"Not really." He folded his arms over his chest.

"What's Cindy doing? Working today?"

He barely suppressed the wince from hearing her name out loud. "No idea."

"You two are having a baby." She glanced over her shoulder to make sure no one was eavesdropping. "Don't you have stuff to do to get ready?"

"There was one thing I wanted to do, but she blew me off."

Annie's gaze narrowed. "I could use a cup of coffee. And I strongly suggest that you join me."

"Why?"

"It's suddenly clear to me why you came to help me out."

"Enlighten me."

"You're feeling an overwhelming urge to unburden yourself. And I'm willing to listen." She nodded emphatically. "You know the drill."

"Doctor's dining room," he said with a sigh.

Annie looked over at the charge nurse, pointed to the door and mouthed the word coffee. The nurse gave her a thumbs-up and a goodbye wave. He fell into step beside her and they rode the elevator down to the hospital's first floor. After walking past the lobby and outpatient registration desk, they turned left and opened the door to the dining room. He was relieved to see it was empty.

"You pour the coffee. I'll get the carbs." She grabbed a couple small plates and put a token slice of cantaloupe beside cookies, coffee cake and muffins.

Nathan wondered how she could put away that much food and still stay so petite. That was simpler than trying to figure out why he felt so screwed up.

Annie picked a table by the window and sat. "I love the cookies. Want one?"

Nathan set two cups of coffee on the pristine white tablecloth, then took the chair across from her. Food was the last thing he wanted. "I'd rather chew off my arm."

"That response to a simple and courteous question contains a disproportionate level of hostility. Want to tell me what's going on with you?" She held up a hand. "And before you try to say no and brush me off, let me remind you—this is me. You can run, but you can't hide."

Her directness was one of the things he liked best about her. So he'd see that and raise her. "I found out that I'm having a son."

"Oh, wow." A soft expression turned Annie's blue eyes tender. "A little Nathan."

"Yeah." He grinned and for just a moment all the other complicated crap was pushed to the background.

"Someone to carry on your name."

And just like that it all came rushing back. "Maybe."

"What maybe? There's no question that Cindy is having your baby. The right of succession has been secured. No?"

"I asked her to marry me."

Annie stared at him, the coffee cup frozen in midair halfway to her mouth. She set it down. "So that's what you wanted to do to get ready for the baby. And she blew you off."

"Pretty much." It was actually a relief to get that off his chest. Maybe confession really was good for the soul.

"So what did you do wrong?" His partner narrowed her gaze on him.

And just like that confession didn't feel quite so self-righteous or satisfying. "Why would you automatically assume it's my fault that she said no?"

"This is me. I know you—the good, bad and ugly. It's not a newsflash that you're not the brightest bulb in the social chandelier. After all, you didn't recognize Cindy when you talked to her outside the hospital. As the story goes, you hit on her. Why is it a stretch to ask how you messed up proposing to her?"

"What's to mess up? I asked her. She seemed excited."

"And then?"

He shifted on the padded chair. "I pointed out all the reasons that it made good sense."

"Be still my heart," she said, fluttering her hand over her chest.

"What? She said, 'thank you, no.' I'm the wronged party here. It's not rocket science."

"You're right," she agreed. "Love is a lot more complicated."

"Love has nothing to do with it."

"That's where you're wrong. Love has everything to do with it."

Nathan refused to confirm that her words eerily echoed what Cindy had said. "In case you forgot, I'm the guy who doesn't believe in love."

"That's a bunch of crap. And you've got it bad." Pity flickered in her eyes. "Otherwise you wouldn't be here on your day off. And the NICU staff wouldn't be wondering what's up with you."

"There's nothing wrong with me."

"Nothing that can't be explained by the fact that you're in love with the mother of your child." When he opened his mouth to protest, she held up her hand. "Save your breath. I've heard it all before. I'll grant you that love is something you can't see or touch. It can't be explained by facts, experiments or data from trial studies. It just *is*. Loving and being loved in return is a miracle and can bring great joy if you're smart enough to hang on."

"Hang on to what? You just said it's not tangible."

"Not in your world." She patted his arm sympathetically. "Your childhood wasn't about emotional growth. It was more like guerrilla warfare. Duck and run."

"A parent's responsibility is to raise their child to function independently."

"And yours accomplished that. But the way they did was more like teaching a baby to swim by dropping them in the deep end of the pool and walking away. It's no thanks to them that you turned out as well as you did."

"That's a compliment, right?"

"Yeah." She picked up a cookie and broke it in half. "The fact that you're a man of science and preaching that there's no rational way to explain love is just your way of being afraid."

"As you so eloquently pointed out, I'm not the brightest

bulb in the social chandelier, but I'd have to guess that's not a compliment."

"I'm your friend. I tell the truth. What you take away from it is up to you. But I'm fairly sure that you're afraid to admit you're in love because when it didn't work out for your parents, you were the one who got hammered. Your reaction to that pain stimuli is avoidance of the offending behavior."

That wasn't news. She'd told him this on numerous occasions, but it always bounced off before. Not this time. Maybe because he was ready to listen and learn. Maybe Cindy had made the difference, laid the groundwork.

"How did you know Ryan was the one?" he asked, wondering about her husband.

"That's easy." Oddly, her eyes filled with tears. "The sex was better than good. The chemistry unquestionable. I knew it—we—were becoming significant, so in the interest of full disclosure before we got to the point of no return, I told him that I couldn't have a baby."

"What did he say?"

"That children were very essential to him and he wanted to be a father. My heart just stopped because I figured it was over. That had happened to me before." She brushed at moisture on her cheek. "Then he said that DNA wasn't the most important part of parenting and there were an awful lot of kids in the world who needed good homes. But there was only one of me and he wasn't willing to let me go. He couldn't imagine his life without me in it."

"And that's when you passed the point of no return?"

"Oh, yeah. I was already in love with him, so that just put the icing on the cake." She turned serious. "I want you to be happy, Nathan. Break the pattern. Take a chance."

He wasn't sure he could do that. She'd zeroed in on his

core belief. It wasn't called *core* for nothing. His deepest truth was that loving someone destroyed everything.

He didn't know if it was possible to break that pattern.

Chapter Fifteen

Nathan got out of the shower, dried off and dressed. He had another day off and nothing to do with himself. Going to the hospital was out of the question. Annie would have him in for a psych eval. Which probably wasn't such a bad idea.

He couldn't stop thinking about Cindy. He wanted to be with her, know how she was feeling, that she was okay. She was sexy and sunny and funny and sweet. There'd been a black hole in his life since she'd refused his proposal.

But love?

Maybe he *was* crazy. He still wanted to marry her—even more than when he'd asked. Not seeing her was driving him nuts. What confused him most was that it wasn't all about the baby. And then he smelled bacon, which convinced him beyond a shadow of a doubt that insanity had set in because no one ever cooked bacon in his house.

He followed his nose to the kitchen, where he found

Shirley standing at the stove, a fork in her hand in front of a pan sizzling with frying bacon.

"What are you doing?"

She glanced over her shoulder and smiled. "What does it look like I'm doing?"

"That's a trick question, right?"

"How can it be a trick?" Shirley's smile didn't falter.

"If I say it looks like you're cooking, you'll say I'm crazy, need my eyes examined, or both." He pointed at her. "Or living in an alternate reality. You're wearing an apron. It has sunflowers on it."

"Well, good morning to you, too. Can't a mother cook breakfast for her son?"

Not in his universe.

"I'm not aware of any laws against it. But this is you we're talking about." He walked around the kitchen island and studied her carefully. "Are you all right?"

"Fine." The smile disappeared but not the cheerfulness.

That was oddly disconcerting. She removed the bacon from the frying pan and placed them on a plate with paper towels, then blotted the crispy strips.

"Would you like hash browns with your breakfast? Or toast? I can do either. Or both."

Frowning, he moved closer and touched the back of his hand to her forehead, checking for fever. "Are you sure you're not delirious?"

"Don't be silly." The Stepford smile was back. "How do you like your eggs? One or two? Or an omelet with vegetables? That would be healthy."

"Stop it," he demanded. "Shirley Steele has never been the domestic type. Who are you and what have you done with her?" Then something else occurred to him. "Or you want something."

"I do. But it's not what you think," she added quickly.

"How do you know what I'm thinking?"

She sighed. "I was sort of hoping this was one of those show-don't-tell moments. But before your head explodes, I guess I better explain."

"I'd appreciate that." He thought about moving a safe distance away but figured holding his own wasn't really a problem.

"I had an epiphany, Nathan."

That's when he did take a step back, then stared at her. "Now I'm really weirded out. And more than a little afraid. Strangely, that wasn't particularly reassuring."

"Maybe you need coffee." The sunshiny expression disappeared, replaced by exasperation that was more Shirley-like.

For some reason he found that comforting. "That would be good."

She poured him some, then looked a little sad. "I don't even know what you take in your coffee. What kind of mother am I?"

"Black is fine." He took the mug she handed him, uneasy now with the way she was acting. "What's going on with you?"

"I need to apologize to you, Nathan."

"Why? Did you burn down the guest house? Paint the walls black?" He smiled at his attempt to cut the tension, but she didn't return it.

"I was a terrible mother. Correction: I still am. I'm self-absorbed and selfish. When your father cheated on me—and make no mistake, it was me he left, not you—I was so completely devastated that I simply couldn't think about anything else. Not even you, I'm ashamed to admit."

"It's okay. I turned out all right."

"No. I mean, yes, you're fantastic, but what I did is not

okay." She met his gaze, her own filled with remorse. "You should have been my primary concern and I'm so sorry that I wasn't there for you. And boarding school." She shook her head. "Ironically that decision was made based on what I thought you needed. I wasn't a positive force in your life under the best circumstances, but when your father left, I just fell apart. I truly believed you'd be better off away from me. What I didn't see until recently was that your world fell apart, too. And you had no one."

For a nanosecond he was that lonely boy again, removed from everything familiar and dropped into an environment so foreign it might as well have been the moon. He didn't know anyone and no one knew him. That was probably the worst. He'd been bewildered and unhappy, but no one had noticed.

Until now. Why?

"That was quite a speech," he said.

"Not a speech. It's from the heart, although I wouldn't blame you for thinking I don't have one." She shrugged. "I'm trying to undo the harm your father and I did to you. He's no longer here, so it's up to me."

His father had died ten years ago. Because the man was a nonpresence in his life, it hadn't left much of an impact. This unexpected change in his mother made him sad for the first time. There was no way to know what a relationship with his father might have been like.

"I'm fine. Don't worry about me."

"I can't help it." She poured herself a mug of coffee and wrapped her hands around it without drinking. "If you were fine, you'd be able to admit that you're in love with Cindy Elliott."

"That subject is off limits." Just hearing her name felt like a punch to the gut.

"Love *is* real, Nathan. If it weren't, your father's rejection wouldn't have hurt me so deeply that I had to hide from life. From you." Her voice caught, but she swallowed hard and continued. "Love exists. It isn't always reciprocated, but it's as real as the heart pumping blood through your body right now."

"Okay."

Nathan didn't know what else to say. She was right. Everything she said rang true and made sense. Especially the part about hiding. He'd been using science and work to dismiss the reality of the emotion and then to hide from it in case he was wrong. Like Annie had said, it was all crap.

"I have a feeling there's more of me in you than your father." Sympathy shadowed her eyes. "When you love, it's deep and forever."

He wasn't going to confirm that he'd just figured out he took after her. "I'm sure my DNA contains characteristics from both of you."

"It's okay to talk to me about your feelings."

"I appreciate that." But he couldn't go there. Not yet.

She tilted her head as she studied him. "Why didn't you tell me the baby is a boy?"

There was only one way she could know that. "You talked to Cindy."

She nodded. "Because you were not acting at all like yourself. I was worried and figured Cindy was the reason. As it happens, I was right. She told me you asked her to marry you. And that she turned you down flat."

There was that fist-to-the-gut feeling again. "She had her reasons."

"She doesn't think you love her," Shirley confirmed. "I think she's wrong, but, along with your fractured childhood, you're still struggling with your guilt that your feelings for Felicia weren't enough."

His gaze jumped to hers and he saw no recrimination there. Only sadness. "Cindy told you?"

"Everything. And for the record, there's no reason to protect me. I'm always on your side. No matter what. What happened to your wife was incredibly tragic. But it's not your fault." She looked down for a moment. "Unlike what you're doing with Cindy."

"What does that mean?"

"All I want is for you to be happy. I'm pretty sure Cindy is the key to that. But you're afraid to take a leap of faith and believe in love."

Taking his breakfast order. Pouring coffee. Wearing the damn apron. It was all to show him that she cared. Food equals love. And then everything clicked. It might be an alternate universe, but he liked it here.

"So that's why you made bacon."

"Now you're cookin'." She grinned. "Your future happiness depends on righting the past. It's my fault your impression of love is screwed up. I'm more sorry about that than you will ever know. Someday I hope you'll be able to forgive me. But now that I've made you aware of the problem, you have to take control. If you mess things up with Cindy now, Nathan, that's on you."

Right again, he thought. The words were invasive therapy to his ailing soul.

He grinned at his mother. "I like my eggs over medium. Hash browns. And wheat toast."

"Coming right up."

She started to turn away, then stopped and met his gaze. "I do love you, son." There was a sheen of moisture in her eyes. "The words sound rusty to me. Probably to you, too. But I promise to practice every chance I get. You'd better get used to hearing them."

"Okay."

"Now, about Cindy—"

He held up a hand to stop her. "I concur with your diagnosis. My resolve is renewed and I will take appropriate steps to get the desired result."

"Then I'm glad we had this little chat and cleared the air."

"Me, too." More than he could possibly tell her.

"For what it's worth, Nathan, I've done your astrological forecast." She shrugged. "Don't look like that. I needed the practice. The thing is, I saw nothing but good things. All the stars and planets are saying love is on the rise. Even the asteroids are—"

"Good to know," he said.

Shirley nodded. "I'm probably the last person you want to hear advice from, but the appropriate steps with Cindy might get a better result if a romantic gesture was included. A really, really big one. That could be just what the doctor ordered."

And it was exactly what Nathan had been thinking.

Cindy pushed her housecleaning cart down the empty hall toward the elevator, really starting to feel the extra baby baggage she was carrying. She planned to work right up until her due date because she couldn't afford to lose the money. In fact, she was worried about how to make ends meet while she was on maternity leave. But then there would be child care expenses when she went back to work.

Marrying Nathan would have solved the problem. Unfortunately it would have created a bigger one. Living without love wasn't really living at all. So, she'd be poor and if not deliriously happy, at least not miserable with a man who buried himself in work to avoid her.

But maybe he would consider a small loan to tide her over. "Cindy. Wait up."

She glanced over her shoulder and saw Harlow. When her friend caught up, she smiled. It was a relief to put her sadness away for a little while. "I heard about the haircut. Very cute."

Harlow automatically touched the sleek, shiny brunette bob. "Yeah? Not too short?"

"No. It's perfect for your heart-shaped face. Sophisticated. Flattering, yet with a hint of sexy."

"You make me sound like a bottle of wine."

"Mysterious, yet bold—"

"Stop." Harlow held up a hand. "Where are you off to?"

"I'm on my way to the NICU." And maybe one day soon she would figure out how to stop hoping to see Nathan there.

"Good. I'm glad I caught you then," her friend said. "Have you heard the rumors?"

"Which one?"

"That you're pregnant."

"Not a rumor. I am pregnant. You know that," she said, putting her hands protectively over her abdomen.

Harlow nodded, green eyes intense. "Well, people are starting to wonder. Is she putting on weight? Or is that a baby bump. Hospital talk about you has gone viral."

In spite of the unease trickling through her, Cindy tried to look unconcerned. "Don't people have better things to do?"

"Well, yeah." Her friend shrugged. "But in between saving lives and getting sick patients well, we love to talk. And you're the current hot topic of conversation."

"Good to know."

"The thing is, Cindy, you need to be ready if

someone confronts you. And they will." Harlow looked very anxious.

"Even though it isn't their concern?"

"Yeah, well, people have a funny way of deciding what is and isn't of concern to them. You can still put them off and keep them guessing, but not for much longer. Then the questions will really start flying."

"Like who the father is," Cindy guessed.

"Bingo." The other woman nodded emphatically, but it didn't shake the worry out of her expression.

"What should I say if they ask me if I'm pregnant?"

"In my opinion as your good friend, the truth would be best. But spilling the father's identity is up to you. I just thought you should know. I really have to run. It's time to start second-round treatments." Harlow gave her tummy a quick, reassuring pat. "Keep the little guy safe. Forewarned is forearmed. Be prepared."

"I appreciate the heads-up."

Her friend started to walk away, then said, "Mary Frances is planning a baby shower. Have you registered yet?"

"No. I'll do it soon."

"Good. How about tonight? We'll have dinner first. My treat."

"In that case, you're on."

"Gotta run."

Cindy watched her friend pick up the pace, then disappear around the corner. She stopped at the elevator and pushed the up button. As she waited, thoughts of her baby's father raced through her mind. She missed him so much. The sudden loss left a hole in her life that could never be filled, not even by the baby. Not completely.

Nathan had so many wonderful qualities. Good-looking, smart and sexy, but so much more. He was kind. And a sense of humor lurked beneath that pretty face. He was noble, dedicated to his work and the tiniest human beings that found their way into his capable hands.

And that's when she knew what she would do if directly confronted about who had fathered her baby.

The elevator arrived and she wheeled her cart through the opening, then pushed the button for the second floor, where it quickly stopped. She got out and headed for the NICU. Stopping in the hall outside, she stepped into the suit and snapped the buttons over her tummy. Her friend's warning had come none too soon. There was very little doubt about her condition.

Bracing herself as best she could, she went into the unit. Automatically looking for Nathan, she was disappointed that he wasn't there. His partner was. Annie was chatting with one of the nurses when she noticed Cindy. She smiled and waved and Cindy returned the greeting before starting her work.

She focused on her job and pushed everything else out of her mind as she picked up discarded packaging from medical supplies. Then she gathered the full bags lining all the generic trash containers, avoiding the ones marked "biohazard" or "contaminated."

She scooped up used linens, then dusted, nearly home free when Barbara Kelly cornered her. To anyone looking on, they were two employees having a casual conversation, but Cindy could feel the vibes. None of them good.

"Hi, Cindy."

"Barbara." Here we go.

"How have you been?"

"Really good. Thanks for asking. You?" Deflect, Cindy thought.

"Not bad." The nurse pointedly lowered her gaze. "What's new?"

And there it was. She was on the spot. To tell the truth

or dodge the issue for a little longer. But maybe this was a good time to get it out there with Nathan not present. He was a doctor, a neonatal specialist who existed on a different plane of existence. If by chance the subject came up some other time in his presence, he could reveal as much or as little as he wanted.

Cindy met the other woman's icy, blue-eyed stare. "I'm pregnant, Barbara."

"Congratulations." There was nothing positive in her tone. "Who's the father? Anyone I know?"

Way to be subtle, Cindy thought. "This may come as a shock to you, but that's none of your business. And it was a rude question."

Barbara shrugged. "Everyone wants to know. But nobody had the nerve to ask."

"How heartening that there are still some people with manners."

Any pretense of civility disappeared and blatant hostility slithered into the other woman's gaze. "Do you really believe you can—"

Just then Nathan walked in. His jeans and white cotton shirt were a clue that he wasn't here for work. He scanned the unit, clearly looking for someone, and Cindy's heart started hammering. The blood rushed to her head, drowning out every other sound.

Finally he glanced in her direction and looked like a predator who just spied his prey. Without hesitation, he walked over and said, "I need to talk to you."

Barbara smiled warmly. "Dr. Steele, what can I do for you?"

"If you'll excuse us, I'd like to speak with Cindy privately."

"Really?" She sounded shocked and disapproving.

Nathan glared at her. "Yes, really."

Cindy was pretty sure Nathan had just put his name at the top of the baby daddy list. Right now she couldn't think about the consequences of that. It was too wonderful just to see him.

"Hello," she said when they were alone.

"Cindy, I know communication isn't one of my strengths. It's unfamiliar to me and I've made mistakes. I'll probably make more. So before I begin, you should be aware that my heart is in the right place."

"I've never doubted that."

"Actually, you have," he pointed out.

"Okay. Maybe at first. Then I got to know you." And love you. She looked at the earnest expression on his face and her heart went all soft and mushy and protective. "Here's the thing. The pregnancy just went public. Pretend you're chewing me out for something then run, do not walk, to the nearest exit. Then no one will know you're the father of my baby."

"I want the whole world to know you're the mother of my child." He stared at her as if she had two heads. "This is the last time I'm going to say this. I *will* be here for you. Always. Publicly. You're the only one who matters to me. If you'll give me another chance, I promise you won't regret it." Then he waited for her to respond. When she didn't, he said, "I wish you'd tell me what you're thinking."

Who could think? "Oh, Nathan—I don't know what to say."

Intensity darkened in his eyes as he said, "Words are highly overrated anyway."

Then he bent and scooped her easily into his arms. She sucked in a breath and threw her arms around his neck as he carried her through the silent NICU while everyone stared open-mouthed. Just before he walked out into the hall, she heard the sound of muffled clapping.

It was a moment.

More than that. It was the most romantic gesture ever.

He took her around the corner to the waiting area, which was empty. Then he set her on her feet and pulled her against him. Seconds later, he kissed her. His mouth was soft, warm, insistent, and her knees literally went weak. Her toes curled and trembles traveled everywhere until she tingled all over. He was so right. When he communicated like this, words were highly overrated.

She had no idea how much time had passed when he finally lifted his head and smiled down at her. She only knew that the emotion so clear in his eyes made her as breathless as his kiss.

"I love you, Cindy."

She'd never expected to hear those words, and they rated really high in her heart. "You do?"

"Yes."

"What changed your mind?"

"I had a talk with Shirley—"

"Your *mom*," she said pointedly.

"Right." He grinned and loosened his hold but didn't let her go. "Long story short, I've been an ass. And I've been wrong. Love *is* real. I see it and touch it every time I look at you and hold you in my arms. I can't see or touch my soul, but I know it's there. As surely as I know it will wither and die without you in my life."

"Oh, Nathan. I love you, too."

"I'm counting on that. Because I'm really hoping that you'll reconsider my marriage proposal what with me not being able to live without you and all."

"Better wed than dead," she whispered, quoting from the movie.

"Pretty much," he agreed.

"Okay, I'll marry you." She smiled up at him. "But only because it's the logical thing to do."

Epilogue

"Is he as beautiful as I think he is?" Cindy stared in awe at the baby in her arms.

"He's the most beautiful baby I've ever seen." Nathan was sitting on the hospital bed beside her, his arm around her and their son, holding them both close. "But we have to find a manlier, more masculine way to say that."

Alexander Elliott Steele.

Cindy hadn't thought she could be any happier than the day she and Nathan were married here in the chapel at Mercy Medical Center, but she'd been wrong. Having their baby made them a family and it was just perfect. She watched him watch the baby, and the love in his eyes was tangible.

He met her gaze and smiled. "I didn't think it was possible to love you more, but seeing what you went through to have our child was just…I don't even have the words."

"I know exactly what you mean." She leaned her head on his shoulder and he pulled her closer, kissing her temple.

She was still sore from giving birth the day before, but the joy of holding her son made the discomfort disappear. The experience was painful and scary but the most awesome thing she'd ever been through. She was strong and would have made it alone, but having Nathan there, encouraging and supporting her was the most beautiful thing. She would never again doubt that he was in it for the long haul. The fact that she knew how much he loved her was a gift beyond price.

She'd thought once that they did everything backward—sex, baby, attraction, love and marriage. But it had all happened in just the right order because they'd actually fallen in love at first sight.

"Hey—" It was a whisper from Shirley who stood in the doorway of the hospital room. "I was hoping Alex would be awake."

"Not now, but it won't be long," Nathan said. "The time will come when we'll treasure these quiet moments."

"I treasure them all now," Cindy said.

"Well, I have a surprise for you and you might want to wake the baby for this."

"Hello, Steele family."

Recognizing the familiar voice, Cindy dragged her gaze away from her son and saw her brother Harry. Her eyes filled with tears because she hadn't known he was coming. "How did you get here?"

"Airplane. Nathan arranged it. Shirley picked me up at McCarran." His dark-blond hair was a little longer than when she'd seen him at her wedding, and he was more muscular than a year ago when he'd gone off to college. He was nearly as tall as Nathan and so handsome. Their parents would be extraordinarily proud.

"Hi, bro." Nathan grinned. "Thanks, Mom."

"Happy to help," she said.

"Hey." Harry walked over to the bed and leaned down to kiss Cindy's cheek. "Hi, sis."

"I'd give you a big hug, but my arms are full."

He grinned down at the baby. "My nephew is a good-lookin' dude."

"He's not a dude," she protested. "But he is beautiful. Would you like to hold him?"

Harry looked horrified. "I think I'll wait until he's a little bigger than a football."

"Coward," she teased. "You've got to man up."

"Don't pick on your brother. Some of us are late bloomers." Nathan had taken naturally to the role of big brother.

Together they'd visited Harry at school in California and he'd come to Las Vegas for long weekends. Her two favorite men had hit it off really well. Now there was a third precious man in her life.

"Well, I'd like to hold him." Shirley moved to the other side of the bed and held out her arms. Her son passed over his son and the new grandmother's eyes went soft and exquisitely tender. "He looks just like you when you were born, Nathan."

"How can you remember back that far, Mom?"

"A mother never forgets."

"I can understand why." Cindy wasn't sure when her husband had dropped the first name and started calling her mom, but that came naturally now, too.

She smiled at her brother. "Harry, wait till you see the mural Nathan's mother painted in the baby's room."

"It's trains and planes and cars right now," Shirley said to the sleeping baby, as she slowly moved from side to side. She tenderly kissed his forehead and said, "But when you get older and we know what you like, I can change it. You can help with the design. We'll talk."

And wasn't that a miracle? The woman who'd run from love had embraced the tender emotion along with her son. Together they'd learned to open up to each other and to her.

After the wedding, Shirley had moved into Cindy's place with their blessing. She and Nathan hoped that the spirit of love permeating the house where she grew up would work as well for his mother as it had for them. And at the astrology store she'd met a handsome, retired Air Force Lieutenant Colonel who was definitely showing interest in Shirley Steele.

But, whatever happened, they were a family now. She and Nathan. Shirley. Harry. And now Alex. This precious baby boy had brought them all together. The sun, moon, planets and stars had aligned on the side of them falling in love.

Cindy and her Dr. Charming had found their fairy tale happy ending.

* * * * *

Silhouette®

COMING NEXT MONTH

Available February 22, 2011

SPECIAL EDITION

REQUEST YOUR FREE BOOKS!
2 FREE NOVELS PLUS 2 FREE GIFTS!

SPECIAL EDITION
Life, Love and Family!

YES! Please send me 2 FREE Silhouette Special Edition® novels and my 2 FREE gifts (gifts are worth about $10). After receiving them, if I don't wish to receive any more books, I can return the shipping statement marked "cancel." If I don't cancel, I will receive 6 brand-new novels every month and be billed just $4.24 per book in the U.S. or $4.99 per book in Canada. That's a saving of at least 15% off the cover price! It's quite a bargain! Shipping and handling is just 50¢ per book in the U.S. and 75¢ per book in Canada.* I understand that accepting the 2 free books and gifts places me under no obligation to buy anything. I can always return a shipment and cancel at any time. Even if I never buy another book, the two free books and gifts are mine to keep forever.

235/335 SDN FC7H

Name	(PLEASE PRINT)
Address	Apt. #
City	State/Prov.	Zip/Postal Code

Signature (if under 18, a parent or guardian must sign)

Mail to the **Reader Service:**
IN U.S.A.: P.O. Box 1867, Buffalo, NY 14240-1867
IN CANADA: P.O. Box 609, Fort Erie, Ontario L2A 5X3

Not valid for current subscribers to Silhouette Special Edition books.

Want to try two free books from another line?
Call 1-800-873-8635 or visit www.ReaderService.com.

* Terms and prices subject to change without notice. Prices do not include applicable taxes. Sales tax applicable in N.Y. Canadian residents will be charged applicable taxes. Offer not valid in Quebec. This offer is limited to one order per household. All orders subject to credit approval. Credit or debit balances in a customer's account(s) may be offset by any other outstanding balance owed by or to the customer. Please allow 4 to 6 weeks for delivery. Offer available while quantities last.

Your Privacy—The Reader Service is committed to protecting your privacy. Our Privacy Policy is available online at www.ReaderService.com or upon request from the Reader Service.

We make a portion of our mailing list available to reputable third parties that offer products we believe may interest you. If you prefer that we not exchange your name with third parties, or if you wish to clarify or modify your communication preferences, please visit us at www.ReaderService.com/consumerschoice or write to us at Reader Service Preference Service, P.O. Box 9062, Buffalo, NY 14269. Include your complete name and address.

USA TODAY *bestselling author Lynne Graham*
is back with a thrilling new trilogy
SECRETLY PREGNANT, CONVENIENTLY WED

Three heroines must marry alpha males to keep
their dreams…but Alejandro, Angelo and Cesario
are not about to be tamed!

Book 1—JEMIMA'S SECRET
Available March 2011 from Harlequin Presents®.

JEMIMA yanked open a drawer in the sideboard to find Alfie's birth certificate. Her son was her husband's child. It was a question of telling the truth whether she liked it or not. She extended the certificate to Alejandro.

"This has to be nonsense," Alejandro asserted.

"Well, if you can find some other way of explaining how I managed to give birth by that date and Alfie not be yours, I'd like to hear it," Jemima challenged.

Alejandro glanced up, golden eyes bright as blades and as dangerous. "All this proves is that you must still have been pregnant when you walked out on our marriage. It does not automatically follow that the child is mine."

"'I know it doesn't suit you to hear this news now and I really didn't want to tell you. But I can't lie to you about it. Someday Alfie may want to look you up and get acquainted."

"If what you have just told me is the truth, if that little boy does prove to be mine, it was vindictive and extremely selfish of you to leave me in ignorance!"

Jemima paled. "When I left you, I had no idea that I was still pregnant."

"Two years is a long period of time, yet you made no attempt to inform me that I might be a father. I will want DNA tests to confirm your claim before I make any decision about what I want to do."

"Do as you like," she told him curtly. "*I* know who Alfie's father is and there has never been any doubt of his identity."

"I will make arrangements for the tests to be carried out and I will see you again when the result is available," Alejandro drawled with lashings of dark Spanish masculine reserve.

"I'll contact a solicitor and start the divorce," Jemima proffered in turn.

Alejandro's eyes narrowed in a piercing scrutiny that made her uncomfortable. "It would be foolish to do anything before we have that DNA result."

"I disagree," Jemima flashed back. "I should have applied for a divorce the minute I left you!"

Alejandro quirked an ebony brow. "And why didn't you?"

Jemima dealt him a fulminating glance but said nothing, merely moving past him to open her front door in a blunt invitation for him to leave.

"I'll be in touch," he delivered on the doorstep.

What is Alejandro's next move? Perhaps rekindling their marriage is the only solution! But will Jemima agree?

Find out in Lynne Graham's
exciting new romance
JEMIMA'S SECRET

Available March 2011
from Harlequin Presents®.

Start your Best Body today with these top 3 nutrition tips!

1. **SHOP THE PERIMETER OF THE GROCERY STORE:** The good stuff—fruits, veggies, lean proteins and dairy—always line the outer edges of the store. When you veer into the center aisles, you enter the temptation zone, where the unhealthy foods live.

2. **WATCH PORTION SIZES:** Most portion sizes in restaurants are nearly twice the size of a true serving and at home, it's easy to "clean your plate." Use these easy serving guidelines:
   - Protein: the palm of your hand
   - Grains or Fruit: a cup of your hand
   - Veggies: the palm of two open hands

3. **USE THE RAINBOW RULE FOR PRODUCE:** Your produce drawers should be filled with every color of fruits and vegetables. The greater the variety, the more vitamins and other nutrients you add to your diet.

Find these and many more helpful tips in

YOUR BEST BODY NOW
by
TOSCA RENO
WITH STACY BAKER

Bestselling Author of
THE EAT-CLEAN DIET

Available wherever books are sold!

NTRSERIESFEB

HARLEQUIN *Presents*

USA TODAY *Bestselling Author*

Lynne Graham

is back with her most exciting trilogy yet!

SECRETLY PREGNANT CONVENIENTLY WED

Jemima, Flora and Jess aren't looking for love,
but all have babies very much in mind...and they may
just get their wish and more with the wealthiest, most
handsome and impossibly arrogant men in Europe!

Coming March 2011

JEMIMA'S SECRET

Alejandro Navarro Vasquez has long desired vengeance after
his wife, Jemima, betrayed him. When he discovers the
whereabouts of his runaway wife—and that she has a two-
year-old son—Alejandro is determined to settle the score....

FLORA'S DEFIANCE (April 2011)
JESS'S PROMISE (May 2011)

Available exclusively from Harlequin Presents.

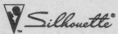

Sparked by Danger, Fueled by Passion.

CARLA CASSIDY

Special Agent's Surrender

There's a killer on the loose in Black Rock,
and former FBI agent Jacob Grayson isn't about
to let Layla West become the next victim.

While she's hiding at the family ranch under Jacob's
protection, the desire between them burns hot.
But when the investigation turns personal,
their love and Layla's life are put on the line,
and the stakes have never been higher.

A brand-new tale of the

Available in March wherever books are sold!

Visit Silhouette Books at www.eHarlequin.com

SRS27718